Tonino Benacquista, born in France of Italian immigrants, dropped out of film studies to finance his writing career. After being, in turn, museum night-watchman, train guard on the Paris–Rome line and professional parasite on the Paris cocktail circuit, he is now a highly successful author of novels and film scripts. Bitter Lemon Press introduced him to English-speaking readers with the critically acclaimed *Holy Smoke*.

Other books by the author published by
Bitter Lemon Books

Holy Smoke
Someone Else

FRAMED

Tonino Benacquista

Translated from the French
by Adriana Hunter

BITTER LEMON PRESS
LONDON

BITTER LEMON PRESS

First published in the United Kingdom in 2006 by
Bitter Lemon Press, 37 Arundel Gardens, London W11 2LW

www.bitterlemonpress.com

First published in French as *Trois carrés rouges sur fond noir* by
Éditions Gallimard, Paris, 1990, revised 2004

This book is supported by the French Ministry for
Foreign Affairs, as part of the Burgess programme
administered by the Institut Français du
Royaume-Uni on behalf of the French Embassy
in London and by the French Ministry of Culture (Centre
National du Livre); publié avec le concours du Ministère
des Affaires Etrangères (Programme Burgess) et
du Ministère de La Culture (Centre National du Livre)

ïi institut français

Bitter Lemon Press gratefully acknowledges the financial
assistance of the Arts Council of England

A CIP record for this book is available from the British Library

ISBN 1–904738–16–8

Typeset by RefineCatch Limited, Broad Street, Bungay, Suffolk
Printed and bound in Great Britain by
Bookmarque Ltd, Croydon, Surrey

ARTS COUNCIL ENGLAND

To Mosko, the painter.

"Juan Gris, the Spanish cubist, had convinced Alice Toklas to pose for a still life and, with his typical abstract conception of objects, began to break her face and body down to its basic geometrical forms until the police came and pulled him off."

Woody Allen, "A Twenties Memory"

"These are just my *painter* friends who killed themselves, all with considerable artistic successes behind them or soon to come: Arshile Gorky hanged himself in 1948. Jackson Pollock, while drunk, drove his car into a tree along a deserted road in 1956. That was right before my first wife and kids walked out on me. Three weeks later, Terry Kitchen shot himself through the roof of his mouth with a pistol... Yes, and Mark Rothko, with enough sleeping pills in his medicine cabinet to kill an elephant, slashed himself to death with a knife in 1970."

Kurt Vonnegut, *Bluebeard*

1

Thirty-five paintings, practically all the same: indescribable black scribblings on a black background. Obsessive, sick.

The day they arrived at the gallery I unpacked them one by one, going faster and faster, wanting to see the surprise and the splash of colour. At first glance everyone thought they were sinister. Even Jacques, my colleague. He's the master picture-hanger, I'm just his apprentice.

"We're pushed for time, young 'un. Doors open in twenty five minutes!"

The director of the gallery only gave us four days to set up the exhibition, all the paintings and three monumental sculptures which nearly did Jacques's back in. Strips of torn steel soldered together, piled up to twelve feet high. Two whole days getting them in position, with two of us at it. I can remember the look on the movers' faces when they delivered them. "Can't they do stuff which fits in a lorry, these useless artists?" Removal men often have trouble, with contemporary works of art. Jacques and I do too, even though we're used to it. We don't always know how to take them, these pieces. Literally and figuratively. We may think we're ready for anything, but we never know quite what's going to appear from the back of the articulated lorry.

Twenty to six, and the private view officially starts at six o'clock. The champagne is chilling, the waiters are all done up in their ties, and the cleaner has just finished vacuuming the five thousand square feet of carpeting. And we always have a last-minute problem; it never fails. But it takes more than that to panic my colleague.

"Where are we putting it?" I ask.

That's the problem. Hanging thirty-five homogenous paintings all in the same family is easy. But there's one little lost orphan amongst them. When I unwrapped it I thought at first that it had got in there by mistake, and that I'd already seen it somewhere else, in another collection. Unlike the others, this one is very colourful with lots of bright yellow and something dazzling about it, an academic portrayal of a church spire emerging from surrounding colour. It's lighter, more cheerful, you could say. Joyful even . . . but I don't think that's a term approved by the upper echelons of the art world.

We kept it till last. The gallery director, the eminent Madame Coste who specializes in the 1960s, has breezed through without helping us out.

"That painting's a problem, I know, it doesn't sit well with the others. Find it a discreet corner where it can breathe a bit. Go on, I trust to you, see you later."

A discreet corner . . . How would this little yellow thing show up amongst all these big black ones? They were quite nice, actually, but terribly aggressive.

Jean-Yves, the restorer, can't stop laughing at the sight of us going round in circles. He's lying on the ground with his white gloves on, touching up the corner of a painting that was damaged during the setting up. *He's* almost finished.

"Only a quarter of an hour left!" he yells to wind us up a bit more.

Visitors are pressing their foreheads against the glass

door, invitation in hand, and already drooling at the thought of the canapés.

"Try over by the window," Jacques says.

I hold the painting up at arm's length. He stands back a bit to see if it works.

"Hmph . . ."

"We've only got ten minutes," I tell him.

"It's still hmph."

He's right. There's an unfortunate contrast between the spotlights and the daylight. The Minister may be coming to the private view, and if we're found here like a couple of idiots with a painting still in our hands Mother Coste will have a fit. It reminds me of the time we got a piece from Australia two hours before the opening. It was in a wooden trunk, fifteen bottles filled with varying amounts of water; it was called "Shark". No photo, no instructions, and the artist was at the Biennale in Sao Paulo. The visitors were starting to scratch at the door. In a terrible effort of concentration, Jacques tried to get inside the artist's head. Click: if they were arranged in a particular order, the water level in the bottles created the outline of a shark, jaw, dorsal fin and tail. We finished just in time. Everyone admired that particular piece – and I admired Jacques.

He's walking in circles, furious and calm at the same time. Jean-Yves has finished his touching up and is sniggering again.

"Hey, you're quite a double act, you could entertain the gallery . . ."

"Shut it," Jacques says serenely.

He draws a hammer from his tool belt and takes a hook from the pocket of his overalls.

"I've got it, young 'un."

He hares off and, carrying the painting, I follow him as best I can into a room where there are already four paintings. He takes two down, puts one back up, paces round, takes the others off . . . they're all on the floor, I can tell this is heading for disaster, he swaps two over then feverishly reverses the decision. Liliane, the attendant, comes by, key in hand, and warns us that she can't delay the opening. Jacques doesn't listen to her; he carries on waltzing to a rhythm even he doesn't understand. An expanse of wall has just appeared, he plants the nail without even measuring the height.

"Go on, hang it there," he tells me.

I hang the painting and look all round the room. Everything is on the wall; the black ones are lined up at the top end and the yellow one is on a "reverse" wall, you don't see it as you come in, but only as you leave. Isolated, but there all the same. I don't even have to check it with the spirit level.

Coste comes in, all fidgety and dolled up in her evening dress.

"That's great, boys, you deserve a glass of champagne. But go and get changed first."

With our overalls and our hammers, we look pretty untidy. Jean-Yves comes over to the yellow painting and looks at it very closely.

"It's a real problem, this picture," he says.

"We're well aware of that."

"No, no, there's something else . . . I don't know what it is . . . A mixture of oils and acrylics . . . it'll never last. And there's something weird about the spire, don't know what but . . ."

"People can paint with whatever they like, can't they?"

The first visitors are coming slowly into the room.

"Does this picture have a title?" Jean-Yves asked me.

"I have no idea."

"Odd . . ."

4

With her firm smile, Coste asks us if we could leave. We do as we're told.

Ten minutes later, all fresh and clean, we meet up again – Jean-Yves, Jacques and myself – by the reception desk where Liliane is frenetically handing out catalogues to journalists. The words "Etienne Morand Retrospective" are written in white on a black background. A waiter offers us a glass each. I decline.

"Why do you never drink?" Jacques asks.

The hall is filling with the usual hubbub, and people are gathering round the enormous sculpture in the foyer.

"I don't like champagne."

And that's not true: I love it, but after six o'clock I have to have an absolutely clear head. It's going to be a long evening, not here but not far away, just up the road. It would be too complicated to explain all that to them.

Jean-Yves looks up from the catalogue and closes it.

"The yellow painting's called *Attempt 30*, and it was Morand's last piece of work."

"Why his last?"

"He died not long afterwards, of cancer. And there are no others called *Attempt*. It's odd to paint nothing but black and then to finish with yellow."

"Oh, that's all part of the impenetrable mystery of the creative process," I say. "God knows what goes on in a painter's mind. Especially if he knew he had cancer. It didn't stop him making sculptures with a blowtorch, so why not use a bit of yellow . . .?"

But Jean-Yves is right: the painting is odd. What intrigues me more than the colour is the image. All the rest of Morand's output is completely abstract, and then there's this extraordinarily precise church spire . . . I really feel I've seen that combination of

5

colour and subject before. It's funny, it's as if the painter wanted to conclude his work with a denial of everything he had done before, with a hint of . . . a hint of life. . . But I don't have time to ponder this: it's time.

"Aren't you going to stay?" asks Jacques.

"I can't."

"You never stay. After six o'clock you whisk out of here like a whippet! We don't see you for dust! One day will you tell me what you do after six o'clock? Are you in love?"

"No."

"What is it, then?"

I start my life, that's all. My life happens somewhere else: it starts after six pm and ends late into the night.

I take my coat and give a general wave. I'm always bored at private views, anyway. Liliane asks me to come by tomorrow to fill in a form with my hours and get my pay. A fond wave to the whole team and a long good-bye to contemporary art. Now I'm concentrating on my own art.

Monsieur Perez, the concierge, sees me leave.

"So, youngster, off to find your friends!"

"Yup! See you tomorrow!" I say to cut any conversation short, as usual.

And it's over . . .

I come out of the gallery and head quickly towards the Rue du Faubourg-Saint-Honoré. The days are getting longer, the streetlights are not yet lit. Good old February, especially the end of the month. A bus passes and I cross the street on a green light. I cut across the Avenue Hoche and pull up the collar of my coat; it's a stubbornly cold winter. In the Place des Ternes the flower market is getting prettier by the day, and the staff at the brasserie throw out binfuls of oyster shells,

6

it's still the season. I'm in a good mood this evening, and I'm going to bring the house down.

On the Avenue Mac-Mahon a Renault 5 beeps at me; I never use the crossings – never mind.

I'm there.

I look up before going in, just to see the huge sign to the temple. My temple.

ACADEMIE DE L'ETOILE

I take the stairs up to the second floor to get to the room. I take a deep breath, wipe my hands on the front of my coat and go in.

The lights, the sound, the smell, the coming and going. . . I'm at home. Benoît and Angelo give me a welcoming squeal, the players perched on the mezzanine look down at me, and I raise my hand high. René, the manager, pats me on the back, and the waitress Mathilde takes my coat. People are playing, smoking, having a good time. I need this, all this explosive life, after hours of concentrating on nails and picture hooks. The audience are not the same brand of people you get at private views. Here, they don't think about anything, they even forget the game, they cheer and heckle or they can even stay silent for hours. And I'm like an addict who becomes himself again after the first fix, at nightfall. And happy with it too. The neon lights are on over every billiards table except for No. 2: it's reserved. I spot a boy getting up from his chair shyly and coming over towards me. I don't know why I think of him as a boy when he's at least my age – early thirties. He barely opens his mouth, but I cut him short straightaway, still staying as polite as possible, though.

"We were meant to meet at six, weren't we? Listen. . .

I'm really sorry but this evening there's a game with the second-ranked French player. I'm not playing, but I really don't want to miss it. I've got you here for nothing . . ."

"Uh . . . it doesn't matter, we can put the lesson off till tomorrow," he says.

"Tomorrow . . . ? Yes, tomorrow, and, in return, I won't charge you for it. At about six, like today."

"That's fine . . . but this evening, can I stay? I mean . . . can I watch?"

"Of course! You should really make the most of the opportunity and book a table to get some practice, to do a series of 'breaks'."

To make this clearer, I starting positioning the balls that René has just brought over.

"No more than eight inches between the whites, and – with the red one – vary the distance: start off with it a hand's width from the one you want to strike. Don't worry about playing for position for now."

"What is 'playing for position'? You've already told me but I've . . ."

"It's when you play a point and try to get all the balls as close to each other as possible, to prepare for the next point. But we can do that a bit later, can't we?"

I play the stroke as slowly as I can and hold my position so that he can memorize the movement.

"The most important thing is to stay absolutely parallel to the baize, I can't stress that enough: the slightest angle, and you've had it, okay? You strike the upper part of the ball with a tiny bit of sidespin to the left and you're rolling."

I don't feel like going back over all the different phenomena hiding behind that one word "rolling". Not again, it took me a good hour in the last lesson.

And you can get to the point where the expression doesn't mean anything any more, they either feel it or they don't, and it comes to them gradually. The boy doesn't look very sure of himself as he picks up his brand new cue, runs a line of blue chalk over the tip and puts the balls back in position. I turn away so as not to put him off.

Everything looks ready at No. 2. René has just taken the cover off and is brushing the baize. Langloff, the champion, is screwing his mahogany cue together over in a corner. He lives in a far-flung suburb and hardly every comes to Paris, just for the national championships or exhibition matches, and sometimes, like this evening, to visit his old friends. His game is a bit austere with no flourishes, but his technique won him the title three times. He was thirty-six back then. Every time I see him play I steal something from him: a mannerism, a gesture, a shot. It will take me years' more work to get to that level, that's what René tells me. But he can tell it's coming.

In fact, I haven't come just to watch: I know that Langloff likes playing three-way games, and René has promised to suggest me for this evening's match. I've been thinking about it all week, that's why I was in such a hurry when I left the gallery.

René is talking to Langloff. I can see what he's up to; he's talking to him about me. I cross my arms and stay sitting on my seat, looking up at the ceiling. It isn't easy playing with a much younger player. I would completely understand if he refused.

"Hey, Antoine! Come over here . . ."

I jump to my feet. René does the introductions, and Langloff shakes my hand.

"So, are you the child prodigy? René tells me you're pretty tough for a youngster."

"He's exaggerating."

"We'll see about that. How would you like a three-way game?"

How would I like it? How do you think!

This evening I really mustn't let my friends down. I shake hands with an old boy who spends all his time holed up in here but hasn't played for two years. "My arthritis!" he says when I suggest a little warm-up. He is sixty-nine, and I am sure he would still hold his ground pretty well. And when I think how long he has been playing I reckon that, at thirty, I have another forty years ahead of me. Forty years of learning. Forty years of pleasure, of jubilation every time a point is made. Sooner or later I will put in for the Championship. All I want is to score the points, I want prizes for beautiful shots, I want to be able to do things which defy the laws of physics, I want the mahogany cue to be an extension of my index finger, I want the balls to take up impossible angles, to obey the most absurd orders, for them to be propelled by remote control by my hand and my will. Billiards is a pure universe: everything becomes possible . . . and simple. You never play the same shot twice in your whole life. Three spheres in a rectangle – and everything is contained within it.

My life is here, around this rectangle.

Forty years to go.

Angelo is playing with us. He has just positioned the balls to determine which of us will play first. He has a thick wop accent, and he always says "when it rolls on velvet, you know it's billiards." I take off my watch and ask for a minute to warm up, just to see how the cue is responding. My hands are fine; they know what to do all by themselves. My eyes are getting used to the light that shimmers over the baize and stays within the confines of the table. We can start.

My mind flashes back to my old uncle Basil. I would have liked him to see me this evening, he taught me to play in the first place, in Biarritz. I was eighteen, I could run fast, hit hard and see far. He was on the brink of senility, it took him ten minutes to cross the room at the café, and he wore bifocals. But he only had to pick up his billiard cue and he would show me how you could flirt with geometric perfection: those beautiful spheres knocking together, spinning, dancing balls.

I really was hooked for forty years' worth then.

*

In the last six games I have only got to my feet eleven times. Angelo has left us together, Langloff and myself, for the last two hours. My best break earned me twenty-four points in succession. Langloff watched me with a strange look in his eye: not really worried, more intrigued. We all knew he would put us in our place, but I kept on at him with the determination of a terrier. At one point I even played a variation of a shot he played last year. I thought it was so beautiful that I spent hours practising to get it right. He remembered it, and it made him laugh. I barely heard the cues being drummed on the ground to acknowledge the shot (our form of applause); I was hypnotized. Everything has worked for me this evening, specially the "screw" shots. When I opened my eyes again, the fluorescent lights were all out except for ours, and there were a dozen or so aficionados watching us in silence. Angelo was there, chalk in hand, keeping note of my score with undisguised joy. René had lowered the blinds, as he usually does after eleven o'clock. Langloff concluded the match magnificently on a point off no less than five cushions – well, you have to end on a high.

We all cheered. René switched off the lights over No. 2, and Langloff took my arm to take me to one side.

"You had me going there, young man."

"You must be joking! You were three sets up on me . . ."

"No, no, I know what I'm talking about. René tells me you don't have a coach."

"Well . . . Yes and no . . . I've got René, Angelo and Benoît."

"You need to step up a gear. I've got my last Championship this year, and after that I want a youngster to bring on. You've got what it takes. Trust me."

René comes over to join us and pats my cheek; I don't know what to say. He agrees with Langloff: I'm their great hope in this place.

"Think about it, young man," says the champion, putting on his mottled grey fur cloak. "We could meet up again towards the end of the year. Think about it . . ."

As soon as he leaves the room, René and Angelo thump me on the neck.

"If you say no, you're a loser. With him as a coach you'd be ready for the Championship in a couple of years."

I feel a bit lost: this has come from nowhere. I need to get out to think it all over, in peace, in my bed.

I put my wooden cue away in its case and said goodbye to everyone.

"See you tomorrow."

Once outside, I took a taxi.

As I lay in bed with my eyes closed, the waltzing balls carried on spinning in my mind for some time.

*

I'm not recovering from these late nights very well at the moment; maybe it's because of my bedding. With the pay I get today I can afford to buy a new mattress. The gallery has just opened, and Liliane is all bright and fresh. Mind you, it is eleven o'clock already.

"Jacques has dropped by already, at nine o'clock. He says hi."

Still half-asleep, I sit down near the reception desk, which still has an empty champagne glass on it.

"Did it go on late?"

"Till midnight," she says. "You wouldn't believe how many people there were. How about you, what time did you go on till? Given the state you're in, you must have had a wild time."

The only answer I can manage is a yawn.

"I've drawn up your payslip, all you have to do is check the hours, and I'll go and get Coste to sign it. And that's Antoine off out of here with his money in his pocket, vanished from the face of the earth until we dismantle the exhibition, am I right?"

It's true that I never set foot in this place between setting up and dismantling an exhibition. Jacques is the one who takes care of maintenance, once a week.

"Who do these works belong to?" I ask.

"To the nation. Morand gave them to the country."

To the nation . . . to everyone, in fact. Partly mine too, then. Coste told us she had met Morand when he came back from the United States and that she had very much liked his work. She really wanted to put this retrospective together.

13

"The Ministry of Culture has loaned us the pieces for a month," says Liliane. "When they're dismantled, they'll all go back to the depot. You're pretty keen on the depot aren't you, Antoine?"

Sure, I like it. It's a huge reservoir of works of art, a stockroom for part of our heritage. I work there in the summer when the gallery is closed, in leaner times. It was Coste who pulled some strings to get me the job.

"When is the next exhibition, actually?"

"March 22, you'll have four days to set it up. And, given the type of pieces, it'll be quite a workout."

"What sort of stuff is it?"

"They're installations, objects mounted on plinths."

Bad news ... I fear the worst. I hate that sort of thing, weird objects, African statuettes with personal stereos, toothbrushes mounted on breezeblocks, basketballs in aquariums and all sorts of other stuff. It's the post-Oxfam effect. For three years now, contemporary art has been competing with a bric-a-brac shop. It's the cult of the practico-inert: you look at a tin-opener on a plinth and you ask yourself all those questions you would never ask in your own kitchen. Fine but ... Jacques and I just can't help laughing. I can't count the number of times I've had to tell visitors that the ashtray and umbrella stand were not part of the exhibition.

"Can you keep an eye on things for me for quarter of an hour? I'll go and get your cheque."

This is the usual procedure. I quite like playing the part of the museum attendant, and it means I can wake up slowly. But it actually involves the work of a Titan; you really need an extensive knowledge of inertia. People often find museum attendants funny, they wonder what they're thinking about, or people say that they are in love with one particular piece of work, that they spend their days daydreaming, sitting there for thirty years with their eyes locked vaguely but doggedly onto the same still-life. Usually it's a plucked pheasant and two rather ripe apples on a willow basket. But here it's more likely to be a willow pheasant and a rather ripe basket on two plucked apples.

Out of curiosity, I glance at the visitors' book to read the praise, insults and graffiti left by the guests yesterday evening. By looking through this, even the very day after the private view, you can tell whether an exhibition will do well or not. And it's not looking good for the Morand retrospective. "*Rubbish, and it's the taxpayer who's footing the bill*" or there's "*A beautiful exhibition. Congratulations*" or "*I can do just as well, and here's my address*" or even "*Thirty years too late. Contemporary art doesn't stop in the 1960s!*"

I really like this big white book, it's the only way the general public can express their opinion, anonymously or openly, about what they have seen. The Morand Exhibition won't get ten visitors a day. But people do realize they are taking a risk when they go into a modern art gallery, they don't necessarily expect to see anything beautiful or decent. Otherwise they would go to the Louvre. And those who, like me, don't know much about it, and who manage three shy little steps over towards something impossible to approach ... well, they deserve the right to scribble a little something in the visitors' book.

A man comes in and smiles.

"Is it open to look round?"

"Yes."

"Is it free?"

"Yes. Come on in."

He doesn't even glance at the sculpture in the foyer and goes straight into one of the other rooms. Not hanging about, then. He is wearing the complete panoply of the gentleman farmer. If I had some money I would dress like that: a herringbone suit, almost certainly Harris tweed, a beige shirt, a glossy brown tie, big English shoes and a crumpled Burberry over his shoulder. Let's see when I get my next pay packet . . .

And if Liliane thinks of bringing back a cup of coffee . . . I could leave here on top of the world with a cheque in my hand and a long, lazy afternoon ahead of me. To relieve the boredom, I pick up a catalogue and leaf through it, trying to find the painter's biography.

Etienne Morand was born at Paray-le-Manial (Burgundy) in 1940. After studying at the School of Fine Art he left for New York in 1964, drawn by the Abstract Expressionist movement. He took a close interest in the techniques used . . .

I stop reading abruptly.

A sound . . .

Something crackled.

Liliane still isn't back.

It may not be very important, a spotlight that has fizzled out or the wire stretching under the weight of a painting, but I have to get up. Unless it's that visitor who has decided, as so many of them do, to try and straighten a picture with a little nudge of his thumb. If that's what it is, I will have to follow him up with the spirit level.

I'll have to do a quick round of the room at the end – softly, softly – even though I hate acting suspicious. As I make my way over, the crackling gets louder. I arrive in the room and the man turns round. I scream . . .

"But . . . !! You're . . . you're . . ."

I'm trying to find a word, an insult perhaps, but I don't know what people say in this sort of situation.

He gives one final jerk with the Stanley knife to free the canvas from the gaping frame. The yellow canvas.

I stammer, whispering various words that stay stuck in my throat.

He calmly finishes the job.

I want to reduce the distance between us, but I can't take a single step forward, pacing ineffectually in front of an invisible, insurmountable wall.

Terror . . .

I lean forwards, twice, without succeeding in moving my legs. I need to break through the bricks, but the soles of my shoes stay rooted to the spot. He is getting flustered too, crumpling the canvas and only managing to screw it into a ball under his Burberry. In order to get out he has to get past me, to walk round me or plough right through me; he hesitates, the same wall is stopping him from taking any initiative, then he shakes his head and brandishes the Stanley knife.

"Get out of the way . . . this is nothing to do with you!" he shouts.

I don't know anything about fighting, I ought to jump at his throat or maybe . . . or maybe I should run to the exit and block the doorway . . . shut him in . . .

I really should step towards him, not let him see that I'm at a complete loss, empty . . . my arms are hollow, I can't get them over this wall of terror.

"Get out of my way . . . for God's sake, get out of my way!"

I clenched my fists before taking off and launched myself at him. I clung to his collar with both hands and dragged down on them furiously to try and get him to the floor. He struggled, and I fell with him. Kneeling on the ground, my fist crashed into his jaw, I struck again, then turned my head, and the blade of the Stanley knife came and planted itself in my cheek. I screamed and released my grip, he drove the blade deeper into my flesh, and I could feel my cheek ripping right down to the jaw.

I stayed motionless for a second. A sheet of blood glided down over my neck.

I cried out.

Sputters of blood spurted from between my lips. Then a great gush of it meant I couldn't utter a sound.

Out of the corner of my eye I could see him getting to his feet and picking up his raincoat.

Slow.

I forgot how much it hurt, a surge of anger heaved me to my feet. He started to run. I lurched after him with one hand on my cheek, trying to hold back goodness knows what – the blood streaming down my sleeve, scraps of flesh, I don't know, all I could see was him, his back. I ran a little faster and threw myself forwards to bring him down. He spun round and fell to the floor in front of the sculpture in the foyer. He drummed his heels into my face, something cracked not far from the gap in my cheek, and my right eye closed of its own accord.

With the other eye I saw him regain his balance on his knees and pull himself up on the sculpture's plinth. With one hand he gripped one of the metallic branches and pulled on it to bring the whole lump of metalwork down on its side. He gave me one last kick in the face, I howled like an animal and brought my arms up over my eyes: everything went black.

I forced myself to look up.

I could feel myself slowly receding. I felt the blackout rising in me like a hiccup. Just the one.

But before that there was a brief second in slow motion.

I registered everything at the same time: the silence, the heat, the flow of blood over my body.

And that silvery avalanche which started oscillating slowly towards me as I sank into unconsciousness.

2

Hot.

My throat is tight, here. If I lift my chin up, I might be able to get it out from under the sheet. Then my neck could breath a bit. But that's not the only thing that's wrong here. When I tried to open my eyes I grasped that only one was reacting and even that wasn't doing very well, just a sliver. The other one refuses to unscrew. And then there's also that prickly line along my forehead, a rough strip sticking to the sweat. However much I move my head from left to right, I can't get it off.

Earlier I tried to open my mouth, but not for long. No way I was going to open my lips like that. Now I've got it. I'm pretty sure that there's a bandage stuck over my nose from one ear to the other, it goes from my upper lip to the lid of my open eye. It doesn't smell of anything, luckily.

I can hear sounds, outside. People moving about. I'd like to move too. If I stretched my neck a bit I could see the rest of my carcass.

Not a chance . . . I've never seen a bed tucked in so tightly. To get away from all this for a minute, I levitate a bit towards the ceiling, gently, escaping, gliding, then looking down to try and find out what I might look like.

A work of art . . . it feels strange being the subject of a Cubist painting. The profile crushed across the front of the face, with one eye hanging over a striped cheek in hot, bright colours. I would never have guessed that I would one day know what a Picasso portrait feels like. And it's not great, from the other side of the canvas.

I must have had a lot of dreams. If I close my eyes, I can get back the final images. A viewing gallery with people standing. My throat's too dry, it's going to stop me getting back to sleep. They all stood up at the same time. The referee stood up too, to check that the white ball shot had actually hit the red. It's true that if you don't get right up close you can't be sure it's happened. I know it has. I made it roll along the cushion with just enough side on it to turn a fraction in the corner. With a little nudge from God. I'm having trouble peeling my tongue off the roof of my mouth, and my taste buds are screaming for water. This must be the first time in my life I've been so painfully thirsty. It's pretty rare. At the academy I don't allow myself any beer, I'm worried it will blur my vision, even a little drop.

Something is cooling the top of my forehead. A hand, which has already disappeared. I lift my head and try to open my eye as far as it will go.

A woman.

A slither of woman. She's moving her mouth.

". . . awake! . . . absolutely not . . . gently . . ."

I can hardly hear anything. My right ear is blocked, and the nurse is talking on the wrong side of me. And not loudly. But I really have to get this right.

"Wa . . . taaaaahhhh!"

That sound alone hurts my lips, or my cheek, but I'm not sure what stops where any more. She brings a glass over.

"Don't move."

I can drink by myself, but I let her do it. It's good. I'll go back to my dreams as soon as this girl has left.

I know exactly why I'm in this bed, it jumped into my consciousness like a scalded cat the minute I opened my eye. I've done the rounds of all the pains, and there's not one missing from the register, particularly the one gnawing at my face. How long will it be before I get my sight back in all its acuity? How long? I don't give a damn about the rest, even if I can't talk or can't hear a thing. None of that's really indispensable to me.

A man's face with a half smile. He had better be of some use to me too.

". . . Issssshi . . . ffffford."

"Don't get yourself worked up. Get some sleep, you're still under the effects of the anaesthetic. Is there someone you'd like to see? They asked at your work if there was anyone we should contact in an emergency, but they couldn't find any details. As soon as you can talk we'll try and sort something out."

What anaesthetic? The cheek? And the idiot didn't understand that it's itching terribly under the bandage on my forehead, and he could so easily have lifted it up and wiped the sweat. I'm going to have to do it myself. My right arm has been immobilized, and my left hand is the only resource I have to try and reach my head. But it's painfully difficult. The man takes my arm almost roughly and puts it back down.

"Please don't move. Is something uncomfortable? Is the bandage too tight?"

It takes him three seconds to work out what's upsetting me and to sponge my forehead and temples with a cold compress. I sigh with relief.

22

"You sleep, I'll come back in a few hours. We'll be able to talk a bit."

We'll be chatting in sign language. The anaesthetic he mentioned is the one in my cheek, the whole right side of my face isn't responding at all. They must have stitched me back together. Soon I'll be able to smell the staples. That shit must hurt. Maybe I'll be disfigured. The boys at the academy will have a good laugh. And the gallery will be like a house of horrors. What day is it? Did it happen yesterday or this morning? I didn't hear anything, no sirens, no shouting. I don't remember any moment of impact; I must have passed out just before that great thing fell down. All the different areas of pain in my face are waking up, slowly. They are joining together, in unison, to make a single wound. I've just run my tongue over the inside of my cheek and got a mouthful of fluid. My mouth is raw. But that's nothing. I want to cry out in pain but I can't, I'd like to see what's left of my face in a mirror but I can't open my eyes, I'd like to run my fingers over every scratch but my arms are like lumps of lead along the sides of the bed. I need my whole body. I need to train every day, Langloff isn't going to think I'm any good. He won't want to work with me any more.

My life is somewhere else.

*

"No one to contact?"

"Ngooooo!!!"

"Don't get upset."

If he says that one more time, I'll spit in his face. If need be, I'll tear off the bandages. My left hand has come back, I've managed to scratch myself several times, but the right hand is bound up in a wad of gauze. And this prick in the white coverall is desperate to find someone to come and cry at my bedside. I'm an only child, my parents are in Biarritz, and I don't want to worry them with all this. They're old, they would go and make the journey just because some bastard tried to carve my face up. My father's not the strong type and my mother ... well, she's a mother – enough said.

"No family or a girlfriend? A friend? It might help you. I'll give you a piece of paper, write down a phone number."

Help me what? Scream? Smash this place up?

As he rummages through his pockets he turns away slightly and asks casually:

"Are you left-handed?"

A little surprised I grunt a no straightaway.

"All right. I'll take your left hand and help you write."

Before I can react, he is already in position slipping a pencil between my thumb and my index finger. I can feel my anger rising up my throat, and I growl at him more and more menacingly, but he brings the piece of paper up to my eye. I can hardly see a thing, I've never written anything with my left hand, and I don't want to let anyone know where I am. But I *would* like to disembowel him. The pencil wouldn't be up to the job. I stab the pencil lead manically at the paper and scribble a sequence of incredibly slow zigzags which run out of my control, skid off the edge of the paper and stop when I don't want them to. I still haven't formed a word with my useless hand. This is purely abstract.

When I feel as if I've finished, the pencil slips and falls to the floor. I hope it looks something like what I intended. He reads it:

"Yes, you're in a lot of pain, you're coming round, but I don't understand what you put afterwards, an A, a P, then . . . is this an S?"

Afterwards I wanted to put ARSEHOLE, but I gave up. I wave my hand to avoid the question.

"I'll call the nurse, and she'll give you something. Try not to move too much."

Yes, I'm in pain and I don't know anyone in Paris who might care about it. Is that really all that strange?

"Listen, I don't want to keep bothering you, I'll ask you one last time to be sure you don't want someone, so okay, you're going to close your eye, once for yes, twice for no, alright?"

To get the whole business over and done with I close my eye twice. There, it's over, now they can look after my poor skin; my skull's burning and it even feels as if all my teeth on the right hand side of my mouth have decided to join in. I can't work out how to get away from this mask of pain any more. Give me a jab, send me to sleep, or I'm going to die!

The nurse comes in, perhaps she's going to save me. They exchange a look, I can't see much; he seems to be shaking his head at her.

"Double the dose of analgesics, nurse."

She reaches over to a piece of equipment I hadn't noticed, a bottle hanging in the air. I give a little gasp of surprise. A drip . . . the tube has been inserted in my right arm for hours, and I haven't felt a thing until now.

"It's a tranquillizer and keeps you hydrated," he says.

I try to pull out my right elbow and they both immediately hold it down on the bed. The girl even gave a little "hey!". They look at each other again, without a word, but I do really get the feeling they're saying something to each other. My right hand seems to be answering, in spite of the bandaging. I'd really like them to leave it alone. I don't remember at what stage it was injured.

"Could you call Monsieur Briançon please, nurse."

The doctor takes my blood pressure and another one comes in straightaway, as if he were waiting outside the door. They exchange a few words that I can't hear, and the first one goes out without looking at me. The new one is younger and isn't wearing coveralls. He sits down on the edge of the bed, very close to me.

"Hello, Monsieur Andrieux, I'm Doctor Briançon, I'm a psychiatrist."

A what . . . ? I can't hear very clearly.

"You'll be back on your feet soon, a week at the most. Your cheek has been stitched up. In a couple of days they'll be able to take the bandages off your eyes, and your vision will be quite normal. In five or six days they'll take the staples out, and you'll be able to start talking again. In all you'll be here about a fortnight to make sure everything starts healing nicely. At first we were afraid you were concussed, but we're happy with your ECG."

A fortnight . . . another fortnight of this place? No way. Absolutely not a chance. If I have to, I'll go to the academy mummified, deaf and mute, but I'll go there. I wail at him, but I can tell that my reasoning doesn't hold much water. I would like to ask him some questions, to explain my situation, to tell him I need all my reflexes. Billiards is special, you can lose a lot in a short space of time. I groan again and raise my arms, he gets up and comes over to the other side. I waggle the wad of bandaging to make him understand what I'm really worried about – my right hand.

"Whaaaa . . . ssssappppe . . ."

26

"Don't try to talk. Put your arm back down. Please . . ."

I do as I'm told.

And something starts nibbling at my stomach. A new pain, strange and blank. It was the way he said "please", I knew he really minded, not like the other doctor.

"There was nothing we could do."

My face freezes. Nothing hurts anywhere anymore except in my stomach. Burning like urgent diarrhoea or a bursting bladder. I need some silence.

"When the sculpture fell it severed the wrist completely."

I'm missing something, he said "the" sculpture and "the" wrist, that all seems very precise. And clear. Severed the wrist completely. Severed. Severed completely. Completely. The wrist, severed, completely.

"I'm so sorry . . ."

Mute.

My whole body has just emptied itself. Lava flowed over my thighs. My left eye closed of it own accord. Then opened again.

He's still there, not moving.

There was a prickling feeling in my nose so I've started breathing through my mouth.

"Your hand was too badly damaged . . . it was impossible even to attempt a graft."

He's waiting.

He's wrong.

I'm not a doctor . . . but he's wrong. And I need silence.

My left hand has been fumbling blindly on the bedside table and has found the pencil. Now it's pointing it in the air. He understands, picks up the block of paper and puts it beneath the pencil.

It scribbles shakily, more anarchic doodlings. This

hand is just doing whatever comes into its head, and doesn't give a damn about mine, about my poor dented head which can't transmit a simple order, a word, just one word; and this thankless hand is exploiting the situation, refusing to interpret for me, it won't do as it's told, it's making the decision, choosing this word, its first word. It's taking its revenge, and I'm shaking all the more.

Exhausted, I let it drop.

He has watched our struggle closely and reads:

LEAVE

The door closes without a sound. The prickling stopped as soon as I could let the tears flow.

*

I sat up with a jolt in the night. I could feel nothing except for the hot and cold sweat plastered all over my body and then, almost immediately, there was a sharp stabbing around my navel. A burning between my kidneys. I couldn't hold back my urine. With my mad hand I fumbled all around the bedside table, things fell to the ground, the water jug definitely, judging by the noise, but I didn't succeed in switching on a light. But I really must see clearly, I must see it, I must touch it. It's there, I can feel it right next to me, it wants to come up to my face, to stroke it, to recognize the outline of my nose and dry my eyes. With a sharp tug of my arm I pull it clear of the loop of fabric that was holding my wrist in place. My stomach is burning, the bandage is too tight, I groan, I can't see a thing, my left hand won't be able to undo the pin and the knot, I'm losing my patience, I open my mouth without worrying about the wound, nothing matters any more, I bite and scratch at the wad, tearing away as much as I can, I scream with rage and swallow a spurt of blood, I'm going to see it at last, it's spreading its fingers as wide as possible to help me, from the inside, it's doing its best, the bandage is loosening, and the wad unwinds onto the floor. I shake my arms like a man possessed, the needle from the drip comes out, that's it, the hand is bare, now I can put it in my mouth and lick my fingers, close my fist and bang it on the wall, write down all the words I want to bellow out, in the dark. It brushes against my side, moving like a crazed spider, climbing up my neck . . .

But I can't feel it against my skin.

The light is back on. Two women in white have thrown themselves at me, even though I screamed like a wild animal to keep them away.

And I saw. At last.

I saw that great spider, that feverish, intangible, invisible spider. Spread-eagled on a jagged stump. A spider that only I could see. And which frightened me alone.

3

In order to avoid the Place des Ternes, I got off at Courcelles. As I walked through the Parc Monceau I came across rows of children in blue uniforms, and I realized it was nearly springtime. Along one of the paths I felt I was about to lose my balance so I sat down on a bench. It happens every time I walk in the open air, without walls. Out in the open I feel lopsided. I don't really know why, but it doesn't last long, a few seconds, just time to catch my breath.

My feet are cold. I should have bought myself some boots instead of this pair of loafers that don't even cover my ankles. Boots would mean I don't have to waste time on socks. I've started to loathe laces, and that's not even the first thing you have to do in the morning.

There's a whole load of other things before that.

Masses.

I've only discovered that very recently. There are so many that I have to choose. Mind you, getting up is not as hard as waking up. It's when I open my eyes that the toughest job of the day happens.

As I went up the Avenue Friedland I looked at the time on a parking ticket machine. Half past ten. The summons said nine o'clock.

There's no rush. Since my convalescence, I've learned to take my time. When I came out of the Boucicaut Hospital I thought about going down to Biarritz, to my parents, to spend a month in physical and psychological rehabilitation, but I backed off at the first obstacle: showing myself to them. I didn't even ring to tell them that my chances of becoming the man I would have liked to be were somewhat compromised. So, nothing; I waited at home, like a coward, for the stump to heal. While I was there I learned to swallow my pride and to admit that I was no longer a member of this fast-moving population. I've joined the ranks of the unsightly, the embarrassing and the clumsy. It takes a huge mental effort on my part to convince myself of this concept which is erased as soon as I fall asleep, then I find myself whole again, whole and kind and not thinking of doing any wrong.

April 3. Hospital was a long time ago already. Coste and Liliane came to visit me, they unwrapped a few sweets for me and I waited, patiently, for them to leave. Jacques didn't have the courage, and I'm grateful to him for that.

I automatically stop by Monsieur Perez's booth instead of going straight up to the gallery. He hasn't seen me for more than a month, but behaves as if I handed the keys in yesterday. His smile comes to a sticky end, his eyes won't hold my gaze and flit furtively over my pockets.

"Antonio . . . Busy, busy in the gallery . . . so how are you, Antonio . . .?"

"And you?"

A car pulls into the courtyard, and Perez hurries over to it.

"They'll park anywhere . . . damn . . ."

People I meet now fall into two categories: those who get it straightaway and those who pretend nothing's happened. The first don't know how to dismantle their handshake; the second, cunningly, invent different forms of greeting. They innovate. And I can't think of anyone in Paris who would dare to give me a kiss to say hello.

I've succeeded in delaying the reconstruction three times without a valid reason. Last week, when I received a real summons, I realized I shouldn't take it too far. During my month's convalescence I did it all by myself, my reconstruction.

Reconstruction . . .

If I had lost my hand in a car crash, under the wreckage of some Renault 16, they wouldn't have kicked up all this fuss. But if it ends up pulverized under a hundredweight of contemporary art following the theft of a strange, yellow painting – public property, at that – people are bound to start wondering. The policeman at the hospital told me that I had definitely come through an attempted murder, because I should really have been hit full-on by that sculpture. And I would have been so much happier with the Renault wreck.

What exactly does reconstruction mean? I'm no longer sure whether they have summoned the victim or the witness. Am I going to be forced to act out my hate? To simulate the brick wall which no one will see? To imply an invisible spider? I can still feel my hand. It's hanging there, inside my empty sleeve. They said it could go on for a year, this illusion. The legless try to get up and walk, and are surprised when they fall over. People without arms rest their elbows on a table only to smack their noses on it. With me it's knocking over cups of coffee when my stump bashes into them. Mind you, that's if I've actually managed to make some coffee. And that's only the third activity in an interminable day.

I recognize the policeman who came to see me in hospital. I have already forgotten his name and some bits of his specialist title, I didn't even know it existed, the Central thingy of Thefts of Works and Whatsits of Art. He must be about the only person who can pronounce the thing in full. Lying in my bed, rigid with boredom, I asked him whether he considered murder to be one of the fine arts. He suggested coming back when I was properly awake. The next day he tried to get me to talk about the assailant, and the only description I could provide was that he was slow, polite and dressed like a gentleman. My only recollection. He found it a bit brief.

"Superintendent Delmas," he introduced himself, "we've been waiting for you."

Subtext: for the last hour and a half. I think I'm becoming more and more of a witness and less and less of a victim. Liliane is there too, next to Madame Coste, who won't be rushing through for once. There are two other policemen wandering about the rooms looking at the new exhibition. I was supposed to have set it up. Jacques must have managed it on his own in this great forest of white plinths.

No one has offered to shake my hand all morning. They have all anticipated this moment and have promised themselves they won't make any blunders. Only Liliane attempted any sort of approach, holding her hand out towards my collar.

"Do you want to take your coat off?"

"No."

"You'll get too hot."

"So what?"

I wasn't asked to be an actor. Delmas asked me the same questions as in hospital, but with movements this time. Here, no there, a bit further to the left, and the raincoat, it was under his arm not on, and any finger-prints? You'll find some on the carpeting, I said, with the hand as an optional extra, to make things easier. Where was that hand, actually?

They knew full well what had happened to the sculpture, though, it was stored in the depot along with thousands of other works of art waiting to be chosen by some town hall or provincial museum. That particular one was bound to go and liven up the gardens round a municipal swimming pool somewhere in France. I would probably have found it unnerving to see it here again, upright and threatening. I wouldn't have been able to stop myself studying the branch that amputated me. I really would have preferred the Renault. But the worst of it is that cars like that are put through crushers and made into works of art too. Not to mention the extremist artists who amputate their own limbs in avant-garde galleries in front of a small privileged audience. "Body Art" I think they call it. I have to say I get a bit lost with all these different forms of expression.

Every trace has been cleaned away, some new carpet squares clash slightly with the old ones, some sections of the right-hand wall in the corridor have been repainted.

After a good hour of farce and nitpicking details, the policeman turned to me, but I think he was really trying to get through to the big boss lady.

"We have his description. If this really is someone from the art world, and more particularly the world of contemporary art, we still have a chance. But in my opinion this was commissioned by a collector. Someone wanted Morand's last painting, and someone else got it for him, that's all. If the piece had had enormous market value we could have made different assumptions. But in this case . . . Morand . . . well, who's heard of him? How popular is he? I'll ask our experts to investigate requests and possible collections of this artist's work, but I don't think many buyers would be interested."

He looks casually towards Coste and asks her what she thinks. And, after all, he's right. I mean, I care as much about Morand's bloody popularity as I do about the future of art.

"The bulk of his work comes from the United States. I decided to do this retrospective because I liked the idea of displaying the work of an émigré who – just like any other émigré – was trying to find work in a different country. And Morand grasped straightaway – I mean, as soon as he arrived there in 1964 – that most developments would begin in the United States. I chose works from his last studio in Paray-le-Monial which I visited in his lifetime, a year after his return."

I'm bored. I want to go home. My eyes come to rest on one of the plinths on which a particularly ugly contraption is mounted.

"When, at the time of his death, he left his work to the nation, I just felt it should be displayed, that's all. From the depths of his workshop I selected things that corresponded most closely with the general trends in his work, the black canvases and three sculptures which I believe are a sort of counterpart to his graphic works, but they are radically removed from the American influence."

One by one, I go through every element that makes up this appallingly pretentious oeuvre. Coste drones on with her great speech, so earnest you'd think she was the Pope. She really loved the Morand exhibition, but I'm wondering by what criteria she chose this latest one.

"And then, there was that unique painting called

Attempt 30 ... It was an enigma to me: his very last exploration, a picture in which the subject has its place, a work of denial, I think. That's why I chose it, because it's as if Morand were leaving us with a question. Art enthusiasts, and I mean informed enthusiasts, might take an interest in the decade from 1965 to 1975, because that was when Morand produced a summary of what was to come. But then ... with that one painting ... that, um ... you could call it iconoclastic painting ... I admit I don't understand."

Delmas is taking notes. The boss lady knows about public speaking. She once even gave a lesson on new figurative representations to a minister who punctuated her spiel with a "yes, yes" every now and then. Jacques and I hammered just a little harder than usual at the time.

Everyone is on the move, Liliane, the boss lady, the policemen picking up their files and their coats, I'm aware of a general indistinct movement towards the exit, no one's talking to me any more apart from the superintendent who would very much like to be contacted if any more details happened to come to the surface. At the hospital he told me that he was having a lot of trouble with the Post-Impressionists at the moment. I didn't get to the bottom of why but, idiotically, I pretended to be interested.

That's it.

End of reconstruction.

Alone and surprised by the silence, I wandered through the rooms a little to gather my wits and to start getting used to the idea that no one was interested in my pathetic situation. Over in a corner I caught sight of a sort of construction based on lengths of guttering stacked one inside the other. There were Venetian masks attached to the pipes, hanging in every direction.

A card by the base explained: UNTITLED. 1983. Plastic and plaster.

For a second I almost shouted out at this imbrication of rubbish. In that brief moment I explored all the absurdity of what had happened to me, just a few feet from there.

I looked over towards the gardens and remembered the piles of rust-coloured dead leaves that had covered it the previous summer. Some artist had thought it would be interesting to create a slightly autumnal atmosphere bang in the middle of June. Not one visitor noticed. Apart from the gardener who distanced himself a little further from contemporary art – and he wasn't the only one.

The word "theft" seems to satisfy everyone. At one point I felt like telling them that it all seemed too simple to me. That painting had hardly any value, and if it was stolen then it must have meant something else. It was Coste who said it, and it's so blatantly obvious. That's a job for a specialist, reading what's in a painting, detecting the mysteries within it. It's because of all that that I lost a hand. If they don't find my attacker, I'll die without knowing what that painting was trying to say.

As I go down the steps I realize that I have been sweating. I will have to resort to taking my coat off more often if I don't want to catch too many chills. In spite of my pride.

"I need to talk to you, Antoine. Can you come up to my office . . .?"

I am just about to walk through the gate, and Coste has raised her voice. It's the second time she has ever used my Christian name. The first was when I tinkered with the transformer on a mobile casing which refused to light up. I don't feel like following her upstairs and getting a sweat up again. I need to get out, and I imply this with a rather ungracious shake of the head.

"I would have preferred to talk to you in my office, but I understand that you must be tired with all these difficult questions . . . Well, um . . . don't let's beat about the bush, you won't be hanging any more exhibitions . . ."

I say no. Although I don't really know whether it is a question.

"I'll find someone else to help Jacques. But I don't want to leave you in the lurch."

She leaves gaps between her sentences, and I can't think of anything – not anything – to fill them.

"I imagine you can't keep your summer job at the depot. Do you have any other source of income?"

"I've got a disability pension from Social Services."

"I know but. . . You can't just stay like that . . . without work. . . I thought. . . Well, listen, I'm going to need Liliane to do secretarial work, and I wondered whether I could take you on as our attendant."

"As what?"

"As an attendant, full time."

She can't hide a little hint of excitement as she finishes her announcement. I don't say anything. I couldn't give a stuff. I just wait. I'm cold.

"Thank you."

I don't know what else to say, and she doesn't understand. As I walk out under the porch I wipe my forehead and leave the premises.

Not now.

A little further on, as I turn a corner, I take out the catalogue that I have carefully slipped into one of my coat pockets. I put it down on the ground and leaf through it to get to the right page.

Attempt 30.

I pick it up between my lips, rip it out with a sharp jerk of my head and stuff it into my pocket. The remains of it, sitting by the edge of the gutter, might intrigue a passing tramp. There are all sorts of tramps, even art enthusiasts, even misunderstood painters.

*

Museum attendant, for life. . . As if my life had ever been there, even just for a second. It was well intentioned, mind you. Madame Coste must have told herself that it was one of the few jobs in which you didn't need your hands. That's all. At one time there were even the halt and the lame at the Louvre, with one blue sleeve folded back with a big nappy pin. Nothing new about that. It's all part of the compulsory five per cent of disabled employees.

But that's not important. What is important is what I have in front of me now, pinned up by my bed. On the way home I stopped off at a photocopying place on the Boulevard Beaumarchais to have a colour enlargement made. They reproduced *Attempt 30* for me, eight inches by eleven. The yellow has run a bit, but it will do.

The telephone rings, right by the bed, and I still tend to put out the wrong arm automatically.

"Hello . . .?"

"Monsieur Andrieux, good afternoon, it's Doctor Briançon. Don't hang up. Could I come to see you? It would be easier."

It's his weekly phone call, he's been doing it since I left Boucicaut. He wants to get a place for me at a rehabilitation centre.

"Listen, thank you for carrying on trying like this, but I don't understand why. What you call rehabilitation is . . . is . . . well, for me, it's . . ."

"You really mustn't be afraid of it, quite the opposite. All you have to do is –"

"I don't want to learn how to be one-armed. I won't get back what I've lost. You wouldn't understand."

"Listen, what you're feeling is completely normal. You have to cross a desert, a desert of resentment, of course you do, but you will get out of it."

A what? Now, when doctors start getting all lyrical. . . Why not a mountain of bitterness or a sea of pain? Doctor Briançon and his killing metaphor. . . I'd rather listen to that than have one hand. If I let him carry on with this, I'll be in for the whole medical catechism, like in hospital.

When I hang up I knock over the two big books that were perched on the edge of the table. One of them, the more expensive one, has the corners of a few pages turned down. Three hundred and sixty francs for a great doorstep of a book on the last thirty years in French contemporary art. The doctor's very kind, but I couldn't give a stuff about his sessions. I unplug the phone. He'll run out of energy in the end, no one pushes their preaching that far. What would I want to do in Valenton in the Val-de-Marne with a load of limbless people?

Morand is cited only as an "*exile from the crisis that hit French art in the 1960s*". It's not as clear as what Coste said, but it conveys the same idea. They only devote about ten lines to him in all. In the other book it's half as many, apart from a bibliographical note which refers the reader to an American study in which, apparently, they say a bit more about him. I have also found a reproduction of a 1974 black canvas that was exhibited at the gallery. I have to lie on my stomach to read, given the weight of the book, and it hurts my back. The small of my back will never recover. The catalogue for the retrospective is, in fact, the only relatively complete work on Morand: a virtually incomprehensible preface by Coste about "the mental space of an artist in transit" and a biography which starts its life in New York and dies two lines later in Paray-le-Monial. Nothing I didn't know already.

Or is it?

Somewhere in the depths of my mind I have a couple of convictions that are becoming clearer and clearer, they are slowly gaining ground and I'm leaving them to grow at their own sweet pace. They've been maturing for a month already. Soon I'll be able to formulate them out loud. It could come into the category of what the policeman called "details coming to the surface". Yes, you could describe it like that. But if he knew what was really coming to the surface for me, I think it would give him more to worry about.

The stolen picture first: we have met before, that picture and I. Perhaps not exactly that one but something close to it, created by the same mind or the same school. A copy? A life-size reproduction? I still don't know yet, it's just a ghost, a presence that takes on a little more weight every day. A movement, a colour, that yellow – so light and even. And the subject, a church spire, painted with such precision at the top and with great sweeping brushstrokes across the bottom. It just emerges from a layer of yellow, as if still

41

growing, straining to grow. Around it there is more yellow, but it is more aggressive, a magma, an impending explosion, something is about to burst out, perhaps it already has, perhaps it is the spire itself. And I've already seen that eruption somewhere. I'm sure of it, but I don't know anything about it. The painting poses problems even for a specialist like Coste, so it should quite logically be completely beyond a philistine like myself. I've never visited any other galleries, not even the Pompidou Centre, I hardly know the Louvre, and painting in general has only ever inspired a sort of gloomy contempt in me. I wasn't receptive to it. When I came to Paris I didn't feel like guzzling on national treasures. My great uncle in Biarritz had given me the address of the Académie de l'Etoile, and I went straight there.

Sometimes, when I was hanging exhibitions, I worried about my non-involvement, my lack of feeling, the thing all the catalogues talk about so sententiously. I thought I was sterile and cut off from all these different forms of plastic exploration, all this art with a capital "A", because people say "artist" when they just mean "painter", and "work" when they want to say "painting". I've always refused to say "work", I thought it was indecent and exaggerated, so I said "piece" which was more technical, more neutral. I could feel my own art churning in my insides, a quest for beauty in the kissing touch between three balls, nothing that needed to be looked at in a particular way or talked about at length, and there wasn't a Coste in the world who could have understood that. People who like painting do a lot of talking, and I'm not that talkative. Yes, there have been things I've wanted, things going on inside my head, but without the questions and without the neurotic search for a meaning.

Now I've been amputated from everything, and it's now that the questions are starting to come. Because nothing is going to end like this: I've only just started, on my own, without the experts and the superintendents. The urgent quest for me now is to understand, even though there is no hope of ever restoring the order of things. No one can imagine the damage I have suffered, and all because of a yellow painting that says more than people realize. My forty promised years have been reduced to nothing in a splatter of lemon yellow.

I've seen that painting. And, now that I come to think about it, my unashamed ignorance on the topic can only be an asset. There aren't exactly thousands of places in Paris where I could have seen it. It definitely wasn't in a book – the one in front of me is the first I've ever opened. Any painting or sculpture can only have appeared in the context of my work, and for several days I've been thinking about the depot, the reservoir of art. For the last two years I've spent the month of July there tidying up and inventorying old stuff that no one wants and that doesn't have a hope of ever being exhibited. I've handled hundreds of pieces there, all covered in dust. I'll go over there a bit later and have a look, just in case. If not, I'm sure I'll find it somewhere else; it will take a little longer but I'll eventually work out where I saw that picture.

At lunchtime I went out to buy a typewriter. At first I thought I might hire one but I quickly realized that the thing would be a part of my life from now on. This useless left hand is never going to help me write a letter. So I paid cash. The salesgirl asked me some questions to try and establish which model would best suit my needs and, after a few moments' uncertainty (when she saw the stump which I'd parked very obviously on the counter), she said she was new and that her boss would be better qualified to help me. The boss woman actually was better, and she sold me an electronic machine, a really straightforward one with an automatic return and a key to erase the last character. I started getting to know the thing, and I even thought I could put it to use straightaway:

The letter to the parents.

I have already perfected a few turns of phrase. But the hardest part is getting the paper in, and it often fails. Right now I'm on the greeting – "Dear you two" – slightly crooked but it's my best result so far. Never mind, this letter will just have to be untidy and a bit crumpled, with typos I can't go back and correct: the hardest bit is still to come. None of my phrases say anything, I don't know how to call a spade a spade. My parents are fragile; they had me late.

I rang Jean-Yves again, but he didn't tell me any more about the yellow painting than last time. I asked him to try a bit harder, to remember what he had said about the texture of the paint. "It was just an impression, really, I'm so sorry. . ." He said I would do best to forget it, and when I asked him what he didn't know how to answer.

I've managed to sort out the problem of what to wear a bit more by finding a bag of old clothes, particularly a couple of sweatshirts that you just have to put on and that's it. There's an old worsted wool jacket that someone really tall left at the academy. It's three sizes too big so I can slip it on just like that. By tomorrow I'll have a pair of ankle boots and some trousers with a zip. I just look a bit more scruffy than usual. I'll have to have the front door repaired, till now I've been keeping

44

it shut by blocking it off with something, but with the warm weather coming back the wood will swell, like it did last year. It's a good thing I'm patient.

*

The first time I came to the depot was two years ago. Before setting foot in the place I'd imagined it as utterly sacred, a sort of sanctuary. I thought you had to put on white gloves and adopt a religious fervour to approach this collection of contemporary works that the country has been putting together for over a century. Experts in the plastic arts, critics and advisers have been meeting regularly since 1870 to build up what will constitute the French national heritage in contemporary art. Sixty thousand works to date. Three quarters of the pieces – and the best of them – are actually distributed amongst national organizations, town halls, public buildings, embassies etc. They have all been helping themselves for a hundred years, and now what's left?

Five thousand bits and pieces no one wants, not even the lowliest mayor in the smallest village, for fear of scaring off his electorate of three. Five thousand little abandoned works of art, unloved and unlovely. Paintings, sculptures, engravings, rolled up drawings, "Art Deco" objects and quantities of mysterious gizmos that can't be classified. The paintings and sculptures are kept in different storerooms, but I loved getting lost among the latter: the mixture of periods and styles turned it into a dusty, Baroque sort of jungle. For the first few days I spent hours wandering along those rows of metal shelving several feet tall, overfilled with statuettes; strolling through that amalgam of shapes and colours. A life-size statue of an infantryman in patinated bronze standing facing a giant hand with fingers of red resin, not far from a toaster encrusted with pebbles. Dozens of busts and motionless faces gazing from every corner, following you everywhere. Cardboard boxes filled with things and trailing electric cables, copper snakes, octopuses with blue suckers, and empty chassis. In one corner, a motorbike mounted on a tripod and ridden by a woman in varnished wood. A table set with assorted cutlery and crockery as if the guests had just fled. Hybrid creatures, half man half machine, wearing strips of brightly coloured cloth. A bored Hussar sitting facing something green.

There are five thousand of them. Incomprehensible and oddly touching. And it was somewhere in the middle of the cruel abundance, this glory hole of art history, that I started to understand a thing or two about the sublime and the ridiculous. What lasts and what people prefer to forget. What stands the test of time and what becomes outdated within a decade.

The living number no more than two: Véro and Nicolas, lost in a huge room converted into an office, right next to the hangars. For years now Véro has spent most of her time listing what is in there and particularly what is "on the outside", which is her way of describing the fifty-five thousand works dispersed around the planet. In theory, everything should be inventoried on registers, but every time she opens one that dates to before 1914 it crumbles into dust. The Ministry has created a processing system to put it all on computer but, in the meantime, you just have to use the archives and, as Véro says, "there are gaps". For now the computer is Nicolas. In the ten years he has worked there he has become the depot's memory, its soul. He can recognize a print from more than ten paces and can tell you where to find the bust of

Victor Hugo which was bought in 1934 (usually stuck between a nineteenth-century bronze and a 1955 "kinetic" painting). What I liked about him immediately was the subtle blend of respect for the material and utter contempt for the work.

Véro has her back to me, pouring herself a coffee.

"Where's the Matisse bought in '53?" I throw out.

She turns round, startled, sees me and heaves a sigh.

"At the Algerian Embassy . . . God, you gave me a fright!"

She smiles, then stops smiling, then starts smiling again differently.

"You okay, Antoine?"

"Yup."

"We heard about what happened at the gallery and . . . do you want a coffee?"

"No thanks. Is Nicolas here?"

"Yes, he's showing someone round the hangars, a local official or something like that . . . he wants to decorate the foyer of his offices. He's asked for a Dufy, can you believe it? A Dufy! Here! He'll go home with a cauliflower in gouache, I can feel it coming."

There's a good stock of cauliflowers in gouache, as she says. It was all the rage in the 1920s. Impossible to fob them off on anyone, even the most kitsch-minded underling.

I slump down into an armchair next to her desk that is strewn with paper.

"Have you had any good stuff recently?"

"Pfff . . . they've bought some engravings which are quite fun and a series of seven steel containers each holding forty-four gallons of water, taken from the seven seas. And it's true."

"Do you know where to put them?"

"We've got room for them, you know the place as

well as I do. But what about you . . . are you going to carry on working at the gallery?"

"We'll see . . . and you? How's your inventory coming along?"

"I've been asking for a work placement girl for years. Apart from Nico and me, no one can find their way around here. You could say we're indispensable in this ocean of shit."

Nicolas arrives, moaning.

"Bloody pain . . . he asked me if I had a Braque . . . oh yes, and what else can we help you with?"

He sees me and carries on moaning: "Oh, hello, are you here?"

Over the years he and Véro have become amazingly alike. They adore each other. They drive each other up the wall. They never give each other the tiniest little kiss to say hello in the morning or goodbye in the evening. They adore each other.

"So what did he go away with, our official?"

"Bugger all . . . except a cold. And what do you want, my friend?"

"I'd like to have a little wander round the stock. Will you give me the guided tour?"

Without really understanding, he follows me into the hangar full of sculptures.

"What I really need is some information. Well . . . it's going to be more like a bottle thrown into this ocean of shit. And I'd rather talk to you about this alone."

I trust Véro but I'd rather not get her involved in all this. He watches rather anxiously as I walk round and round a Polystyrene Venus de Milo.

"Go on, explain. . . I don't like mysteries."

"Have you ever had stuff by Morand in the depot, I mean, apart from the things in the retrospective?"

"Don't understand."

48

"Did the Ministry ever buy anything by Morand before he bequeathed his work?"

"Nothing. The first I heard of him was when the retrospective came up."

It's what I expected: if there had been anything else by Morand, Coste would have mentioned it straightaway.

I take out my page from the catalogue.

"You see, I wondered whether you had anything here that looks a bit like this. I know this might seem strange, but I've got a feeling there's a picture very like this somewhere here. There's such a hotchpotch, you never know."

In amongst that hotchpotch, for example, there's a dangerous sculpture that it's best not to leave bits of yourself on.

"We've never had anything by him before."

"I don't know if it's really another painting by Morand that I'm looking for. I just made a connection with the painting that was stolen. It's just a visual similarity, maybe the colour, or a movement."

"A movement?"

"Yes."

"Are you taking the piss? A movement? With all the stuff I've got here? That's like going to the flea market in Saint-Ouen and asking if they happen to have seen a crackled vase."

I realize that's pretty much the problem so I come at it from another angle.

"Yes, but you're not like that, you could even date a picture from the layers of dust on it, you could define the rate of yellowing of a litho print, you're the only person who can see the difference between a Caillavet sculpture and a stalagmite."

He smiles in spite of himself.

"Yeah, yeah, and you're the only person who can talk bollocks like that. I'll have a think about this thing of yours. Are you still at the same phone number?"

"Yes. And I also wanted to tell you . . . this whole thing is my business . . . what I mean is . . . it's personal . . . and the less you know about it, the better."

"Don't worry about it. You don't want me to talk about it, is that it? Not even to Véro? You poor thing, who the hell do you think is going to be interested in this piece of yellow shit . . .?"

*

Attempt 30 and its growing spire. I feel as if I'm experiencing the effort along with it. When I unwrapped it I looked at it more closely than the others, those hopelessly black ones, and then I went on to the next without wasting any time, and the pieces as a whole just swelled the ranks of the dusty, anonymous reserves in my memory. The depot I have in my head, my own useless collection. I didn't suspect anything at the time, but I now know that that spire is being born, you just have to look at it for a while. And it gives you a funny feeling if you think it's never stopped piercing upwards since the day Morand conceived it with a few dashes of his brush. How much time did it take to suggest that pressure? I would say very little. A spit in the ocean. But I may be wrong, to a specialist who can gauge the true work that went into it, it could have taken weeks on end. At the same time, over and above all these questions, I refuse to believe that so many things could have passed me by at the gallery, that I wasted all those hours setting pieces up to look their best without ever realizing that their best was already part of them, intrinsic and meaningful.

I preferred concentrating on what my real life was going to be, the one that started after six o'clock. In that world I was in charge of everything: the hours I worked and the hundred different ways of making the point. Usually there are only two or three for every thousand ways of blowing it. And between those two there is often a choice between beauty and technique, and you choose according to your mood, the score and whether or not there is an audience. And I was very keen on the cheers and the bravos.

The letter to the parents.

How to tell the people who gave you two hands that you are now one short. I can't even picture my mother's face reading those lines. She was reassured when I told her I had regular work at the gallery; she didn't like seeing me leaving with her older brother to hang around some café where people played billiards. My father couldn't give a damn, always lost in great works of literature, he spent his whole career trying to pass on his love of the language to students who showed varying degrees of enthusiasm.

When I write this letter I'd like to avoid complicated words. I'd like to avoid words altogether. To say it without writing it. The word "amputated" feels like the thrust of a dagger to me. Invalid, amputee, severed completely . . . and there are plenty more that are off limits. In fact, what I should be doing with this letter is painting it, if I had the talent and the equipment. Painting is about the only way to represent things that can't be expressed in words. A simple drawing could spare me a great saga that is bound to end up lying to itself.

I would have to paint an uncompromising picture,

with no hope, in harsh colours, showing how everything around me is now damaged. No prospects. Nothing optimistic or pastoral. The inner violence. Expressionism.

Dear you two,

I won't be playing billiards any more now and that should please you, mum, because you always said you can't make a living in the backrooms of cafés. I want to scream at you about my hand. You were worried about Paris, dad, you said it was full of trouble. This afternoon I went into a shop near Bastille to buy a cleaver. A proper butcher's cleaver, I took the biggest one that would fit in my pocket. At the moment no one knows I've got the thing in my possession. In the hopes that my useless hand doesn't betray me when I do come to use it, I send you all my love . . .

Someone's knocking at the door. I peer up from my typewriter and wait for a while before opening the door.

Fist raised, he is preparing to knock again. I should have guessed that Doctor Briançon would come sooner or later to see the extent of my distress with his own eyes.

"Um . . . good evening. Could I come in?"

He got my address from the files at Boucicaut.

"If you want."

He runs his eye over my little dugout. A psychologist's eye? A prying eye? I don't know.

"Would you like to sit down?" I ask, indicating a chair over by the kitchen area. "I haven't got anything to offer you. Oh yes I have, a glass of wine or a coffee."

He hesitates for a moment.

"A coffee, but I can do it, if you don't feel like it . . ."

"No, that's okay, but I want some wine. We'll do a

swap, I'll make the coffee and you can uncork the bottle."

He smiles, as if I've made a real effort to prove willing. He's barking up the wrong tree. Why me? He must have loads of people in a much worse state or much more vulnerable than me. Family breadwinners, children, hemiplegics, paraplegics, every kind of trauma case. Why me? Does he want to tell me about Valenton?

"I like this part of Paris. When I first came to the city I looked for something round here, but the Marais's so expensive."

I don't say anything in reply. He may be good at listening to answers; he's still the one doing the asking. And I'm definitely not opening the debate for him. I pour the ground coffee carefully into the filter and press the button, like a proper little left-hander.

"Have you played billiards?"

What?

I snap my head round.

He points to the cue standing against the bed.

"Is it yours? I don't know anything about it but it's magnificent. Is it maple?"

He's found it, his opening. I take a deep breath before answering.

"Maple and mahogany."

"That must be worth a bit."

I don't understand his methods: a mixture of genuine curiosity and provocation. It's odd, the minute I stop being aggressive, he starts.

"Yes, quite a bit. But that's the charm with a lot of works of art. Beautiful and expensive."

"And useless."

For a split second I can see myself snatching the bottle and smashing it across his forehead. And he has just picked it up to plant the corkscrew into it.

"In the end, I'm regretting my decision," he says looking at the label. "If I'd known you had some Margaux . . ."

I switch off the coffee machine and take out another glass. He pours the wine.

"You're right. If you're going to drink, you might as well have the best."

"Listen to you, Doctor Briançon, you sound like a man crossing a desert of resentment. Shall we cut to the chase?"

Silence.

"Okay, you're right, we can't prowl around the subject for hours. My job is to rehabilitate people with psychomotor disabilities, and in your case there are thousands of things you can do instead of hiding away in your shell. Simple things but they need working at. If you put in the effort, every opportunity would be open to you, you could live normally again, you would become left-handed."

Silence. I let him finish. He'll be out of the door all the sooner.

"There are compensatory phenomena in all forms of disability, and you should concentrate all your work on your left hand in order to recover all your abilities. In the subconscious we all have the same body image, that's why you will continue to appear whole in your dreams for many years . . ."

"Piss off."

"No, let me speak, you shouldn't let this opportunity go, the longer you leave it, the . . ."

"Why me? Tell me why for Christ's sake!"

I have raised my voice. That's probably what he wanted.

"Because there's something about you that I find intriguing."

"Really . . ."

"I get the feeling the trauma is more profound than with any other subject. There's something . . . something violent."

"What?"

"I don't know yet."

After a momentary feeling of surprise I burst out laughing. But the laugh dies a strangled death in my throat.

"The accident itself, for example. . . Losing a hand under a piece of sculpture . . ."

"An industrial accident like any other," I say.

"Oh no, and you know that better than I do. It's the first case they've ever had at Boucicaut. Then there's your stay in hospital, your unexpected reactions like the day I took the stitches out. Your face had already changed but what surprised me was how calm you were, almost serene. It was as if nothing had happened, no pain, no gasp when we drew out the staples, no rejection when you saw the stump you would have to live with, no questions about the future, no distress, no rebellion. Nothing, an absent expression, a mask, a peculiar passivity concerning whatever was asked of you. Except for physiotherapy and rehabilitation. You're going to think this is strange but you're behaving more like someone with third-degree burns . . . there's an attempt to stay motionless, I don't know how to put it . . ."

Mustn't answer. Mustn't help him.

"There is one thing I'm sure of, at least: you're taking the loss of your hand much harder than anyone else I've cared for. And I want to know why. That's actually why I came to see where you live."

He gets up, as if he can feel the surge of hate rising in me.

"Be careful, Antoine. You're on the borderline between two worlds . . . how shall I put this? . . . it's the occupied zone on one side and the free territories on the other. And at the moment you're hesitating . . ."

That seems to be his last point. What could he possibly add to that?

"Is that it?"

He nods, as if to calm things down. As he headed for the door I could see he was assessing my bed-sit again. Like an idiot, I realized I had left the spanking new cleaver lying around, for all to see, sitting on the paper it had been wrapped in. He didn't miss it, that's for sure, I could tell just from the way he said goodbye, with his eyes, letting them linger on mine.

Never mind.

My stubble is beginning to itch. I can't go more than three days without shaving, otherwise. . . Before going to bed I look at myself in the mirror, with my clown's clothes and my neglected face. I see myself as one of those stupid creatures, always looking right at you, so you can't get away from them, the ones that populate the paintings by a young artist whose name I can never remember.

*

This morning, when I was only half-awake, I rushed over to my billiards cue; I wanted to touch it, tighten it up, see it. I realized I was still asleep and my head was spinning from getting up so quickly. The telephone rang and, in my sleepy haze, I recognized Nico's voice, although I didn't understand much of what he was saying. I collapsed back onto the bed.

56

Two hours later it feels as if I dreamed all that.

I haven't even waited for the change from the taxi driver before running to the office. Véro, still with a cup of coffee in her hand, is watching Nico packing some framed engravings.

"You're pretty quick," he says.

"So are you," I reply.

He takes me off into the hangars. I wonder what Véro can be thinking about our little game.

"I spent all night thinking about your yellow thingy. Because when you showed it to me, I also thought. . . Follow me."

He gets asked for connections like this three times a week. It usually happens when he is having his lunch or breaking for a cup of tea.

In the third storeroom, the one where they keep rolled up pictures without frames, he kneels down. I felt him hesitate for a moment, thinking of asking me to help.

"It can only be one roll, I know all the others. And I never look through the things, they make me sneeze."

Some of them are easily more than a century old, and every time I take one out it sends up a cloud of dust and makes me cough. Now I can see why they waited till July to get me to restore some order in the place.

"I used the size as a reference. The Morand one and this one are both eight figures."

"I wouldn't know."

"Eighteen inches up by fourteen across."

I look at it, laid out on the ground. And the shooting pain in my stomach suddenly starts up again.

"So? What do you think? Pretty good work, hey?"

My memory is doing pirouettes.

I'm hypnotized . . .

He waits, anxiously, for my reaction.

A bright red. Treated in exactly the same way as the yellow in *Attempt 30*. I might even be able to remember when I saw this red. It was the first time I came to work here, in the early days I couldn't resist unrolling everything I laid my hands on, just to have a good laugh at all this old stuff. I liked the absurd possibility of chancing across a forgotten masterpiece. But the Ali Baba cave very soon turned into a wasteland. I remember a rat hurtling out of one particular roll.

"It's like it, isn't it?"

I can't take my eyes off it. The paint is a little cracked but there is exactly the same academic application in the way the subject is drawn; this time, though, it isn't a spire but the capital of a column. Everything has changed, the design and the colour, and yet it features the same system, it's from the same mindset. Nico grumbles a bit when he sees me dusting it down carelessly. There is an inscription on the back of the painting. I read it with almost no sense of surprise: *Attempt 8.*

We both stay there, dazed, crouching in a cloud of dust.

"And have you seen this?" he says.

"Yup, it's the eighth in the series."

"No, no, this, at the bottom, on the back."

In tiny letters, in the bottom left-hand corner of the picture there is another inscription that we have missed. Given the position, it could be the signature.

"The Objec . . ."

"What's that there? Is it a T?"

"The Objec . . . tives, is it? It looks like . . ."

I think I have made out the whole of the signature. That's what it says, but is it really the signature?

"The Objectivists."

"Yes!" says Nico. "Objec-ti-vists. But what are they . . . ?"

First and foremost we need to work out how this painting landed up here. I sit on the ground with my back up against the metal upright of the shelving. And I take a deep breath.

"Was it bought?" I ask.

"Of course it was, how else would it have got here? There's even the inventory number: 110 0225," he says, reading the ticket dangling on an elastic band.

I close my eyes for a minute. Just long enough to recover, and to formulate some more questions.

"Right, Nico, can you give me some idea of how much information we can get on something in this place?"

"Hmmph . . . it depends when it was bought. In this particular case I can tell you right away what's on the label: *Attempt 8*, Name of artist: The Objectivists, Size, Type, Date: 1964. If I look through the registers for the inventory number I might be able to come up with more details."

I still haven't opened my eyes.

"Are you pleased with this, Antoine?"

He is proud of his find. But I'm feeling something quite different, something strange. Like a starting point.

I could still walk away.

"Yes, I'm pleased . . . I'm pleased."

I feel a need to get out, just for a moment, to be back in the fresh air, and – more importantly – to buy a Polaroid camera so that I can keep some proof on me that I'm not on the wrong track.

An hour later the photo is in my pocket. Nico doesn't seem all that happy with this precaution.

"Right, okay, now we can really talk seriously. Véro and I are responsible for the depot, we have to know everything that happens here and definitely have to *account* for everything that happens here. And, to be honest . . . we don't want any trouble. This isn't easy to say but, basically, you can take your photo, get the information that you want today and then that's it, I'll roll up the picture, put it back where it came from and shut it away. Now if anyone asks me to find article number 110 0225, I'll get it out for them on the spot. Okay? I don't want to know what's going on, why you're looking for all this and what you're thinking of doing with it. I do know that . . . that you had a hard time back there . . . but it's none of my business. I don't want to worry Véro. Next time you come to the depot, you'll just be coming to say hello. Got it?"

A starting point. Nico has just confirmed that for me.

"Got it."

*

The light has just gone off automatically while I'm still halfway between two floors, and it throws me off balance. I hang on to the banister rail as best I can and climb up slowly, bent forward, with my left arm across my body. Sounds of keys, the light going back on, my neighbour coming down the stairs.

"Do you need some help?"

"No."

"If you need anything, you can always knock on our door, Monsieur Andrieux."

"Thank you."

I have a nasty way of saying "thank you"; it sounds like "who cares?" I'll have to watch that. I don't want the doctor to be right, I don't have any grudge against the rest of the world.

The date on the painting and the date of purchase are the same: 1964. It doesn't mean anything to me except that it was the year Morand left for the United States. Nico looked through the register for that year and didn't find anything else, apart from the month it was bought: September. Which month did he leave French soil? The artist's name has been recorded only as "The Objectivists". He explained that you didn't always get the real name if the artist liked to use a pseudonym. In this instance it must have been a group, although there was no way of knowing how many members it had. There too, you couldn't be sure, it could be a pure invention. You get that with painters, you have to view everything as a bit suspect with them. Morand's name doesn't feature. I don't know whether he might have been a member of "The Objectivists" or just picked up on one of their themes, or perhaps he wanted to pay homage to them. Or maybe he just created them. With contemporary Art you have to be careful. From what I've read on the subject, you get every possible scenario: people who never sign their work, people who sign for someone else, groups who make a name for themselves by trying to stay anonymous. . . It's hard to tell where the profession of faith ends and the publicity stunt begins. I went back to the pages that talk in detail about these groups and reread them in a different light; and it's quite a scrum. They started appearing in '66 or '67 with weird names like the Malassis, Surface-Supports, BMPT and Panchounette Presence. But these "Objectivists" are never mentioned, and I'm not all that surprised because if they had been well known or even minor figures Coste would have said something about them straightaway, she would have made the connection with Morand. But no, we know nothing about his life from the time he left the Beaux-Arts to when he set off for the United States. And yet the nation has bought one painting by these "Objectivists".

What sort of time-span was there between *Attempt 8* and *Attempt 30*? Twenty-two days, twenty-two years, or just twenty-two attempts? Each of them in a different colour, with a new subject every time, perhaps a staircase surrounded by orange, perhaps a door handle in a sea of white. I would have done a billiards cue on a green background, with a couple of white smudges. But I'm not an artist. No one has asked for my opinion. Still, I would have found that much more appealing than the others. The hardest part would have been creating the impression of movement, and you can't improvise that sort of thing.

4

Tourists marvel at the brightly coloured tubing and the visible framework of the Pompidou Centre, but when I come out of the library on the second floor it's Paris that I look at. Those same tourists are happy they can make out Notre-Dame not far away; and tomorrow they will be over there making out the Pompidou Centre with the same enthusiasm. If they climb enough landmarks they might end up establishing a point of view. In the Contemporary Art section of the library I have looked through more books but my research techniques were a bit half-hearted compared to the avidly note-taking students gathered round the table. The Objectivists sailed through history without leaving the least little anecdote for posterity, without the tiniest *nota bene*. I've ended up thinking they didn't exist and that the painting at the depot is a hoax by a student from the Beaux-Arts, perhaps Morand himself. This could be the story: Morand spends six years learning his trade at his college on the Quai Malaquais. To cloud a few issues he invents a group and a concept, just to impress the authorities on the subject he paints an *Attempt*, and it goes down well, he's taken everyone in, one of his paintings is bought and he signs it "The Objectivists". Then he goes to New York because everyone in Paris dreams of SoHo. He forgets France for twenty years, then he goes back to his roots, to Burgundy, where he whiles away the time with a blowtorch. Right at the end he paints another *Attempt*, a reminder of the days when everything still lay ahead of him. That could be his life, this Etienne Morand, artist, stirrer, exile . . . who still remembers the past.

I also looked for books by one Robert Chemin, a former inspector of works of art who has now retired. I found *Chronicle of a Spontaneous Generation*, which I flitted through just so that I would have something to say before meeting him. He agreed to meet me at his own home, at half past twelve. He made quite a point about punctuality, adding: people who have nothing to do with their time are always the latest. To get hold of his name I asked Liliane, she hasn't been able to refuse me anything for a few weeks. She found me the complete list of inspectors who voted on the national acquisitions committee in 1964. Of the twelve names on that jury, seven are still working at the Ministry and the others have retired, and I wanted one of the latter – to try and avoid direct contact with official channels. No one must know that I'm snooping around the national collection. You never know. Delmas might be worried by so much initiative.

On my way down the escalator I remember the media circus when the Pompidou Centre first opened. For or against? Major event or scandal? No one could get away from the subject. The market porters from Les Halles made a rapid exit to Rungis rather than confront such a tricky question. Like everyone else, I was quick to form an opinion . . . which I've subsequently forgotten.

Twenty past eleven. Chemin lives in the Rue Saint-Merri, very close to here. I have time to wander round the National Museum of Modern Art for a bit, for the first time since I came to Paris. I have the choice between the permanent exhibition on the fourth floor and a retrospective on Narrative Figuration on the mezzanine. On the ground floor, behind a notice saying "new exhibition coming soon", I can see two picture-hangers laughing out loud as they turn a painting every which way, trying to distinguish the top from the bottom.

I've moved over towards them, out of curiosity. I heard the older one say to his friend: oh, hang it all, I suppose I have to do this!

It reminded me of some good times.

As I go up the stairs I waggle my right sleeve slightly and push it down into my pocket. You see I don't want to be taken for what I am – a man with a missing hand – even at the risk of being taken for what I'm not – plain rude. I realized rather late that my infirmity was the best visiting card to leave in people's memories, an absolutely first-class distinguishing feature. Not to mention my face, which even I find disturbing, or even my general appearance, like a second-hand clothes dealer who's lost three quarters of his bodyweight. Everything is designed to make me unforgettable.

In an almost simultaneous movement I ring the bell and bend over so that I can put my hand round my left ankle. The door opens, I look up and there he is, surprised to have to look down.

"I twisted my foot slightly on the way up ... it's nothing," I say, rubbing my ankle.

"Um ... Come in, sit down ... Do you need any help?"

"No, no, I'll be fine, I just gave myself a fright, that's all."

The hall is a sort of sitting room, like a waiting room, with a sofa and some armchairs in faded pink, arranged in a circle. I limp a little as I go over to one of them and sit down to take off my jacket.

"Oh, those stairs . . . they're terrible! And I really can't face them any longer with my old legs," he says. "You be careful on your way back down."

The room is very overheated, almost oppressive. I can see a writing desk in a corner with three plaster models of jaws acting as paperweights. A coffee table overrun with magazines, *National Geographic* and *Geo Magazine*; there are even some on the floor, open, spread-eagled, gaping. Newspaper cuttings pinned to a corkboard, photos from the press, I'm too far away to see what they are about.

He sits right opposite me on the sofa. I casually cross my left leg over my right knee, and it feels as if I am sheltering my bad side.

"Thank you so much for agreeing to see me, it's very kind of you . . ."

I wait for a moment for an "it's my pleasure" which isn't forthcoming.

"And . . . well . . . I've recently read your *Chronicle of a Spontaneous Generation*, and, to get a bit more in-depth information, I'd like to know whether the groups which emerged in the 1960s really –"

"Have you read it?" he cuts me off suddenly.

"The *Chronicle*? Yes."

"Are you a student?"

"Yes."

"Are you going to take any notes?"

I get the feeling my visit is going to be shorter than I anticipated.

"I'm interested in the groups, I'd like to base my thesis on the 1960s, seeing the decade through the emergence of these disparate groups of 'angry young men', sort of forerunners of 1968. You've written a book about it, and I wondered whether you could talk to me about it, I have a very good memory, it's that simple."

Silence.

"Yes . . . I see. . . Disparate and 'angry young men', you say. . . Groups like the 'Wait-and-Seers' in '63 or the 'Blue-Greens', who came a little later."

"That sort of thing."

Silence.

"Are you trying to make fun of me? You're confusing Rock 'n' Roll with modern art. . . Neither of those groups ever existed. Who are you?"

Now it's my turn to be silent. I feel as if I have already run away. I stare at the pile of *National Geographics* for a while, then let my gaze slide over to the wall. Should I get up? Should I stay? Before I would have shuffled out looking at my feet, but now . . .

"Well?"

I remember some particularly dramatic matches at the academy. Those gloomy fifteen minutes when you stay pinned to your chair while your opponent succeeds in imposing silence on the room, patiently, and then – just when he consents to leave the floor to you – you get up and do something really hideous and hand it straight back to him.

"Right, okay, I'm not a student, and I don't give a damn about modern art. To me you're not the author of that chronicle, you're a former inspector of works of art, and you were on the acquisitions committee in '64. I went about this the wrong way, I wanted to get you to talk in general terms for a bit, and then to nudge you softly, softly onto the acquisitions committees so that I could squeeze out some information on one or two particular things that I'm genuinely interested in. I don't give a damn about the rest."

"And what is it that you're genuinely interested in?"

Alternating the silences with quick responses, that's what I'd like to be able to do. They must have had slick, tight discussions in those days.

"One group, 'The Objectivists', who produced a painting something like this."

Rather than going to great lengths describing it, I show him the Polaroid – which requires a pretty ungraceful contortion of the whole left side of my body. He reaches over to his writing desk for his glasses and holds them over the photograph like a magnifying glass. He stays bent over it like that for a good while, motionless, screwing up his eyes. I let my gaze wander again and almost forget that I'm here with my quaint lies and my arm ineptly hidden behind my back. In the distance, in the open doorway to the next room, I see a small painting hanging on the wall. It is no larger than the average seascape, with little colour but, in the darkness, it is impossible to make out the image.

"Where did you get this from?"

Instead of answering I hand him the reproduction of *Attempt 30* so that he can compare them. He needs less than a minute.

"No doubt about it, it's the same artist, or someone's been very faithful to his style. And where did you get this one from? Give me at least one answer, it would help me . . ."

"From a catalogue on Etienne Morand. I just want to know if he was one of 'The Objectivists'. Does the photo remind you of anything or not?"

His rotating hand gesture could mean any number of things.

"It's funny . . . seeing this again now. It's more than a memory. 'The Objectivists', you say? It didn't take me long to forget such a stupid name. But this, here, this piece, the red one, I remember this perfectly."

I'm not sure I find this reassuring.

"We were wary of those unruly youngsters who wanted to burn all our icons. They would do anything to overturn values, particularly the legitimizing bodies, as they were called then. That was us, the ministry, the critics, the dealers. Everything I talk about in my book, if you've read it. But when this painting turned up before the committee, we were all a little . . . worried."

"Worried?"

He seems distant, absent, lost in the depths of his memories.

"Well, yes . . . it feels strange to be. . . Yes, worried. . . There was something powerful and spontaneous about it. It had an energy. I don't know how else to put it. I've forgotten at least eighty per cent of what was presented to us, but not this painting. Our deliberations usually went on forever but, that day, not one of us tried to deny the force, the urgency we had in front of us. We voted unanimously."

"And the painters, did you meet them?"

"No, and for a very good reason! Two of us tried to get in touch with them straightaway, to visit their studios, to understand the way they worked, their methods. We were convinced that they were very young, that they were bound to need support. We were prepared to pull strings for them, that was what we were there for, after all. But they just didn't want to know."

He stops to catch his breath. Unless he's heaving a deep sigh.

"Did you meet them? Was Morand one of them?"

"I've just told you that we didn't. And this Morand you're talking about is pretty obscure now so at that time, well, you can imagine. . . On the other hand, we had heard about them before they presented this painting. Three months earlier they made a . . . a contribution, an intervention at the Young Painters' Exhibition. I wasn't there but I wish I had been. They came on the opening night of the exhibition even though they categorically hadn't been invited, they hung their paintings anywhere they could, and handed out tracts that were unequivocally insulting to the art world, and absolutely no one was spared. After thoroughly abusing everyone there, they took their paintings down again and left. And, between you and me, that sort of lightning demonstration became almost commonplace after that, but they set the precedent. So their name wasn't completely unknown the day it came before the committee. We were even rather intrigued when we saw that they were putting something forward. Worried, yes, that's the word. They refused to sign with their own names, or even to have links with any kind of institution. It was the embodiment of 'art for art's sake' and a rejection of the star system, of any speculation about different artists' popularity. Well, you see what I mean, all the movements that appeared a few years later. But this was only '64."

"That's just it . . . don't you think it's a bit strange that these idealistic rebels refused to be picked up by the commercial dealers at the same time as presenting a painting to the nation?"

"Yes, I do."

I wait for a bit more explanation, which he probably doesn't want to give me. He waves his hands as if to say "yes, I know but . . . what do you expect? . . . that's all part of the terrible contradictions of art."

"There must be a reason, isn't there?"

He seems to be irritated that he can't reply, he waves his hands about in a different way and mumbles

70

something indecipherable. I repeat my question again, just as it was – and that is when I feel I have gone too far.

"Now listen, my young friend, I'd like to know why you're perching on the edge of that chair, resting your entire weight on the ankle that was hurting a few minutes ago."

I didn't think, I didn't have time to ponder it and, without my knowing why, my arm has appeared of its own accord. It snapped up like a flick-knife with the naked stump under his nose.

He is trying not to show any surprise.

"It's worse than I thought," he says carefully, getting to his feet, "I think it's time you left, don't you?"

Yes, I think so. I've probably outstayed my welcome. As I stand up I put my stump back in my pocket . . . but there is still something intriguing me.

"Just one last question. Earlier on, you realized straightaway that I was talking rubbish but you still didn't mind trawling through your memories. I'd really like to know why."

He rewarded me with a snigger, though not a cruel one.

"That, my young friend, is very simple. It was something of a pleasure answering your questions from the minute you admitted that you don't give a damn about contemporary art. Because, you see, whatever you may think, you could never give so little of a damn as I do! And it feels good being able to say that from time to time."

"I don't understand."

"I spent thirty years of my life blathering about works of art which got more and more pared down, minimal . . . invisible. Until I saw them disappear. I lost myself and I no longer knew who I should support and why, the very act of putting some colour on a canvas

71

was increasingly suspect, and all anyone could talk about was concepts. In the end emotion was completely forgotten. One fine day I realized there was nothing exciting about it any more, examining an art form that was more interested in establishing its own 'history' than anything else. Nowadays, artists don't paint any more, they compose, they conceptualize, they confirm the fact that no one can paint any more, they put everyday objects on plinths and scream and shout about the end of 'artistic hierarchies' . . . and they theorize about the death of art. Actually, they're just waiting for something to happen. And for a long time I waited with them for someone who would open up the way. Your 'Objectivists', for example, they definitely had something to say in spite of their absurd name, but they disappeared as quickly as they arrived. I ran out of patience and now I couldn't give a damn. Like you."

"Doesn't any of it interest you any more?"

"Oh, you know, I don't know this world and its landscapes. And that's important – the landscapes, the earth, *things*. I've never walked through something beautiful or taken a stroll through lots of colour. Or I must have let it pass me by. I started with the opposite. Monochrome before chlorophyll."

"Do you regret that?"

"Not really. You know, I understood Turner much better when I flipped through an article about Venice. I should have gone there when I still had the strength in my legs. There isn't a single painter, not even Van Gogh, who's succeeded in recreating the strident yellow of the rape fields in Provence. And I've never been there either."

He walks me to the door.

"That's what you claim but. . . I don't know how to say this . . . I saw a picture hanging in the next room. If none of it means anything to you any more, there are just a few square inches which still warrant being looked at."

He sniggers as he opens the door and pushes me out. Before closing the door he gives another snigger.

"The picture you saw is magnificent, it's a portrait of my mother done by my brother. And it's priceless. But, between you and me, it was just as well he didn't pursue his career."

*

Once outside I hurried into the Métro as if there was some emergency, and I spent the rest of the afternoon at the Archives Office of the Paris Biennial Exhibition, another library of contemporary art in an annexe of the Grand Palais. I found everything they had on 1964, particularly the press cuttings for the Fourteenth Young Painters' Exhibition. In one article The Objectivists did get a mention. I couldn't quell a surge of anxiety that stopped me concentrating on an important question: should I steal the documents or copy them? I hovered in front of the photocopier for a minute, then in front of the librarian. She hardly looked at me and completely failed to notice my missing hand. I waited for the man next to me at the table to leave before scrunching everything I needed into the rubbish bin of my left pocket.

As the clock struck seven, I made another attempt at the typewriter. I feel as if I'm getting worse, it takes me a ridiculously long time to get the sheet of paper lined up on the carriage and it's mostly my irritation that makes it take so long. I'm short on patience. My father chose that exact moment to ring and complain about the weeks of silence. I didn't tell him anything in particular while trying to lie as little as possible. I'm a bit worried they will turn up unannounced one day and I wouldn't have the courage then to put my arm up in the air like I did this afternoon. That's actually just what I need, something as clear-cut as that gesture. An overall picture with all the accuracy of a photograph. A cold, clinical vision. A hyperrealist image.

Dear you two,

Imagine a part of the human body that doesn't exist, a smooth rounded extremity that you would almost swear was natural. Put it in the exact place where there's usually an ordinary hand. That's my stump.

Somewhere between a slight feeling of drowsiness and a lukewarm bowl of soup, I let the night creep up on me. But there was no question of going to bed until I had completely unravelled the crumpled paper in my pocket. The telephone rang, and I almost didn't answer, convinced that Briançon was at it again.

"Antoine . . ."

"Nico?"

"I know it's late, I'm still at the depot and I've got something for you. Something big, bring your Polaroid. You're starting to bug me with this business . . ."

Is it the darkness, the fact that I've never spoken to Nico after eight o'clock, or the thought of coming face to face with this something big, but I didn't spark as quickly as he wanted.

"Can it wait till tomorrow?"

"No chance, it won't be worth it any more tomorrow, and hurry up, I want to go to bed, my little girl's waiting

74

for me, and I don't get paid overtime. And bring the picture you took yesterday because this time I'm the one who's going to need it. You'll see what I'm on about the minute you get here. See you."

Just time to pick up my camera, hurtle down the stairs and nab a taxi over by the Place des Vosges. I didn't need my right hand for any of that. But I managed to forget – for the space of ten minutes – that it was missing.

He has thought to leave the door open. The light isn't on; I've never known where it switches on but the spotlights from the hangar of sculptures in the distance guide me on my way. In the darkness I bump into a small trunk and, by some miracle, I manage to save a sort of vase (I don't know if it's a work of art waiting to find its own place or a common jug for watering the plants). If only I knew where the switch was. . . I step over a roll of bubble-wrap lying on the ground next to a frame waiting to be wrapped up. Nico has so little room in the hangar that he squats in Véro's office to make up his parcels. I cross the little courtyard which leads to the store of sculptures that, by contrast, is ablaze with light as if some high-ranking official was expected at any minute. The familiar smell of old wood and fermented resin hits me. I yell Nico's name. I'm not forgetting that it's night-time, not that that changes anything but it adds a dimension, an air of decadence. I take a few shy steps into this disintegrating fortress. A Xanadu.

"Nico. . .? Nico! What the hell are you doing. . .? For fuck's sake!"

The stone faces no longer look bored at all, oh no, they're threatening this individual who has come to disturb their rest. A wan-looking virgin watches my progress with her empty eyes. "After seven o'clock I leave the works in peace," Nico always says when he wants to leave. And it's true that, outside the working day, they seem to want to be left alone. Nothing seems ugly any longer, or pointless, each piece reaches its own threshold of maximum inertia at last, as if just being looked at by visitors forced them to pose.

I head down an aisle outside the range of the light.

And there, as I come round a huge thing in wood, it takes me a while to realize that a set of shelving containing busts has toppled to the ground. A tide of heads has washed up at my feet, earthenware cheeks, dozens of women in greened bronze, in varying shapes and sizes and variously cracked. And on the edge of this wave there is another face that looks even more inanimate than the others.

"Nico?"

I brought my hand to my mouth.

Not far behind me I heard an order.

"The photo . . ."

I didn't turn round straightaway.

The voice, Nico's smashed-in temple, the fear so strong I want to throw up, I thought I was back in that moment that turned my whole life upside down.

"Give me the photo . . ."

The photo. . . I'm well aware that he's going to want more than a photo tonight. Last time he took one of my hands. The time has come to see whether I can really count on the one I've got left.

I didn't turn round, I leaped forward to grip another set of shelving and pull it off the wall with all my strength. I didn't look over my shoulder but the crashing sound ran through me like an electric shock. I raced to the exit, jumping over everything in my way, climbing over cases and leaping over tables. I remembered a row of paintings leading to a door that would get me back to the office. I don't know if he's following me or if he's using the main door to cut me off. After the excess of light and flashes of bright colour, I was plunged back into the shadows of the office. I could tell he was in there too, and I closed the door to make it completely dark. He must be over by the door, trying to find the light switch. In hand-to-hand fighting I wouldn't last long, I remember that from last time (and that was when I had two to match his). He may be armed, I don't know, I didn't turn to look: he may have a gun trained on me, I wouldn't know. It's a big office, by feeling my way I might manage to find something, I don't know what, just while my pupils dilate. His too, mind you, it won't be long before they get used to the dark.

"I advise you to give me that photo."

Yes, it's coming from the reinforced door, the one that goes out onto the street. He doesn't know where to switch the light on. It's my only hope. In case he does find the switch I give the lamp a good kick and then dash over to a stack of pictures.

"You won't be as lucky as last time, I'll make sure of that."

If he were really sure of himself he would head straight for me. He needs to work out where I am too. Even I'm lost, and I know the place.

"And your friend, who works here, he told me you've been somewhat . . . diminished."

He already knew he was going to do Nico in, almost before he hung up. He must have grilled him for quite a while before finishing him off. He came here for *Attempt 8*: Nico got it out for him straightaway and told him everything, my visit, the photo. . . Another trace of

The Objectivists, not counting all the ones I have in my head. He wants to destroy them, all of them, that's why he got Nico to ring.

"You're persistent, but I'll get you in the end."

With great difficulty I manage to make out the things around me. I don't imagine he can see much better.

"Tell me, I didn't really notice earlier, do you have a hook?"

A what?

A hook, that's all I need to rip your throat out. I heard the scratch of a match, and a little sphere of light created a faint halo around him. It just gave me a chance to see his face again and his gentleman's tie. He is trying to make out my outline, huddling between two pieces of furniture.

The little flame goes out.

"You're very persistent."

Another scratch. I can only see his legs now; he has moved forward a good three yards already.

"You and me, surrounded by all these works of art . . . we have the whole night ahead of us."

I can sense his stealthy progress as he brushes past something that snaps like a straw. I manage to crawl into a different position but the Polaroid swinging from my shoulder knocks into a table leg.

Another match, but this time I can hardly see anything.

A scrunching of paper . . . the light becomes much brighter. He must have set light to something. An improvised torch, a print perhaps.

A smell of burning? A crackling sound. Proper flames, something really is burning. He is more than ten yards away from me, I can look up enough to see what he is up to.

He is trying to light a rolled-up picture with his torch.

Attempt 8.

He's actually risking setting light to the place. I'm going to roast like a chicken. For him that's more than a hypothetical solution. With all the stuff in storage here, there could be two nights of inferno before they find me. It would be a spectacular, grandiose fire.

It's almost over, the flames have nearly devoured the painting.

"I'd like something to drink. Some whisky . . ."

What on earth can he mean by that? Maybe nothing. . . Or just that he feels like drinking whisky. I didn't see a gun. I miss my hand, with that I could have hurled a whole table at him, I could have used it as a shield. Or maybe it's inside my head that I miss it. He's right, I've been diminished, and he knows it. Diminished . . . that's the word. Impotent. *Concentrate all your work on your left hand.* I'd really like Briançon to see me right now.

"The only thing I regret here is the quality of the pieces. I thought I would find absolute wonders."

Judging by his voice, he is walking up and down, pacing between the tables.

"It's incredible trying to work out which of these might be the same age as our grandfathers. Does art really go that quickly? Perhaps that's all it is, after all, just a question of time. The people who do graffiti in the Métro might be exhibited at the Louvre one day. What do you think?"

I'm losing him. In what he's saying and, more worryingly, in placing him. The smell of burning is gradually fading. This masquerade can't go on, he will run out of patience. He's talking crap like this to break me down.

"Give me that photo."

I'm breathing clouds of dust. Right now he could be anywhere. I know where Véro's desk is. I feel along the top of it, I do it without a sound. He must have heard, I pick up a pencil and then something slim and metallic. A paperknife.

"Do you miss your hand very much?"

There's one thing I'm sure of, you piece of shit, I'll cut your throat in the end. I'm doing all this for you. If I had known I would see you this evening I would have brought my meat cleaver. It might have given me some courage. Anyway, I need a hand. Maybe not yours, but a hand all the same. You turned me into a physical monster, and the mental equivalent wasn't far behind. That's logical. I don't know what you've got against these Objectivists, but they're all I have left now.

He must be standing over by the main door. I'll never have enough strength in my arm, or the skill to stab him with this crappy paperknife. He might have a razor twice the size in his hand. He's going to have a great time.

Tiny flashes of light . . . he is walking over by the bubble-wrap, the exact opposite of where I thought he was . . . he is very close. To my right . . . very close . . . It's now or never.

I climb onto the table and throw myself onto him, trying to pierce into him, striking at him as best I can but my arm feels empty, bashing his chest but it won't go in, it's dark, my arm is hollow, like a reed, brittle, the blade either slides over him as if stroking him or grates onto the concrete floor. With a bit of light I would be able to see him smiling smugly. I can't slit his throat, I can't even cut him with this shitty little blade in my powerless arm . . .

Not the tiniest little nick. I won't be getting his hand

tonight. I dealt him one last blow to keep him on the ground a few seconds longer. And I fled. Tipping over everything I could as I passed. Once outside I ran blindly through the streets for a long time, with Nico's dead face as my only horizon.

*

I only managed to catch my breath once I was home, up in my apartment. I felt finished. I tried to gather my thoughts, to understand myself, to grasp how I could have seen a corpse – the corpse of someone I knew – and only a few minutes later to have wanted only one thing: to pierce a living man's flesh. Briançon must be right: I'm no longer in the free territories.

*

First thing in the morning I found myself in Biarritz trying to justify God knows what to a couple of mutes. I didn't fare any better in the oral than in the written test. The distance was too huge. I've done my best to drive their expressions from my mind.

Nine-thirty, Véro arrives at the office, the door is open, there's the smell of burning, a charred picture on the ground, upturned furniture, the lights are all on in the storeroom, the shelving is on the floor, busts scattered on the ground, and the rest. I get up to have a drink of water, the cramps in my neck make me twist my head in every direction. The typewriter with an indelible "Dear you two" rolled round the carriage. The coffee machine. My billiard cue. The crumpled pieces of paper spread out over the table. I can't see what is most urgent. Yes I can: putting the cleaver away in the cupboard. I sit back down, get up again, wander

81

round the shower. I wouldn't mind making a phone call, I don't know who to. I can't think of anyone close enough to me to cope with the lament of the vengeful amputee. All of this is because of billiards. I didn't have enough patience for anything else. Lying on my bed, I thought of the pianist who ended up losing a hand like me. Ravel wrote him a concerto for the left hand. That's what it is to have friends.

Soon Delmas will try to contact me. I need to be ready for it. Perhaps that's what is urgent. He's going to talk about Nico and an "attacker". That makes it sound like a profession. And, actually, as far as this gentleman is concerned, I still can't understand how he operates. Methodically or just by improvising? No weapon, apart from his serenity, his patience and some sort of Stanley knife.

I stayed on my bed for several hours, without grappling onto anything coherent. The documents are still waiting, and they'll just have to wait. Véro must be in a bad way at the moment. I'm condemned to spend the evening here, in the same feverish state.

Towards the end of the afternoon, Delmas rang to ask me to come and see him without giving me a chance to quibble about when, and I took this as a release. "In an hour would be best, and don't be too late. . ." From his turn of phrase I realized that our relationship had just gone downhill imperceptibly.

In response I deliberately loitered. But with some excuses: as I slipped my Métro pass into the slot I realized that the world was definitely not designed for left-handed people. It only takes so many little details of that sort to come to that conclusion. Nothing too restricting, no, but it's just a little too systematic. A travel pass – it slides in to the right, like when you open a door or put on a record. Minor things. And it gets you every time. Before I would never have noticed the way things have been conceived. I had a lot of trouble putting my travel pass away in my breast pocket, because right-handed people use the left-hand pocket. Once I had managed to emerge from these musings and to down a beer, I made my entrance at the Investigations Squad and into Delmas's office. The man still hasn't grasped the fact that he can't treat me just like anyone else.

From the flush in his cheeks and the slight twist to his mouth I can tell he has just spoken my name. But he didn't feel he had the right to raise his voice, not yet.

"Don't you know how to be on time?"

"Yes, but everything I do takes twice as long as it would for you. In others words, for me, every hour takes two."

Hey, I could get used to mucking about like that. I stop talking for a moment, so that he can tell me Nico is dead.

"I asked you to come because something happened yesterday which may be connected with what happened to you. Did you know Nicolas Daufin?"

Daufin . . . what, like a dolphin? If only I'd known that when we worked together . . .

"Nico . . . yes, he works at the depot."

I haven't picked up on his use of the past tense.

"He died yesterday in circumstances not dissimilar to your assault."

I don't say anything. I can't think of anything to say. And if he gets the feeling that this isn't news to me, bad luck. I'm rubbish at reconstructions, even emotional ones.

"What sort of . . . circumstances?"

"He was found in his depot under some shelving full of sculptures, but he was already dead when the shelves were pulled over onto him. First the attacker had tried to strangle him with a shoelace, then he struck him on the forehead with a bust. There are also signs of a struggle in the entrance. You know the layout of the depot . . ."

"Yes, I've worked there."

I didn't see the shoelace yesterday, just the blue bruising round the sides of his face. Delmas isn't mentioning the burned painting.

"Do you go back there much?"

"Hardly ever, when I'm in the area, and I'm never in the area."

"What about the last time, how long ago would that have been?"

Danger.

There are two possibilities: either Véro has told him about it or she hasn't. Either way, Delmas is sneaky. The only way I can play this ball is straight down the line, onto the cushion with a little sidespin to the right.

". . . a long time ago. Several months."

"Before or after your accident?"

"Well before it, at least it's a good point of reference for dating things!"

"Have you had no contact, even by telephone, with Monsieur Daufin or Mademoiselle Le Monais?"

"Véro? Do you know Véronique as well?"

"She found the body. Was she very . . . very close to Monsieur Daufin?"

"I never really knew. They got on very well, at the time. How is she?"

"Not good."

"That bad?"

"She took it very badly. She came out into the street

84

and a passer-by saw her collapse. He contacted the police."

There's no fathoming what really goes on between people . . . They weren't related or married. Just work colleagues. Friends. He closed up the depot, and she opened it in the mornings. Nothing ambiguous in their behaviour, no way of knowing whether they had been lovers or whether they still were. Nico said "my little girl" when he referred to his private life. No fathoming it . . .

"You and Daufin have worked together, and the two of you end up under pieces of sculpture a couple of months apart. You have to concede that that's enough to make a connection."

"Yes, there's no getting away from that. Except that I was a bit luckier than him."

"It is Mademoiselle Le Monais who inventories the collection, isn't it?"

"It's taken her ten years already, not to mention the ten still to go."

"Surely not, I've seen to it that the process is speeded up. Personally I've never seen such a shambles. Starting next week we're drafting in a team to record every last grain of dust in the place. We need to know exactly what the attacker was interested in."

There you are . . . she's been waiting for her work experience people long enough, poor Véro . . . I wish them luck, the little new boys. It will be several months before they realize that one pathetic little rolled-up painting has disappeared. Even Véro has never heard of "The Objectivists".

One of his henchman comes in and asks if he wants a coffee. Delmas says no and offers me one. I accept.

"Tell me . . . what do you do at the moment?"

I realize that this is the most important question.

That this is what he got me here for. It takes me a little while to adopt a natural pose, the time it takes for me to snap the sugar lump between my fingers. It's a knack I perform more and more proficiently, and it's my way of showing the superintendent that, for me, the most difficult laws are ergonomic ones. Because the others, the ones that justify his practices and determine my freedom, the ones we apply without knowing it and we violate without any pleasure, the ones that generalize individual cases . . . those laws are hardly anything to do with me.

"Not much. I'm trying to become left-handed."

"Is it difficult?"

"It's slow. What are you? Right-handed?"

"Yes."

"Well, you're with nine tenths of the human race, and you're better off there, because you know about the problems of minorities as well as I do. At the moment I'm trying to make myself a little place amongst the other one tenth. But I already know that I'll never have the benefits of a true left-hander's short circuiting."

He doesn't seem to know what that is. There isn't even time to explain, he's onto the next thing. The man couldn't give a stuff about the short circuit, that hundredth of a second quicker response time which is enough to mean there are five left-handed people in the six-strong French fencing team, and three of the world's top five tennis players are left-handed. And I'll never enjoy that, that tiny advantage. You have to be born with it. But the superintendent couldn't give a stuff about that . . .

"Are you going to work at the gallery?"

"We'll see. For now I just want to wipe all of that out."

After a short, irritated silence, he turned calmly

towards the window. I felt uncomfortable because I could no longer see his eyes.

"I'm going to find him."

No point asking who. It sounded like an impossible challenge, an appointment with fate. Did he say it for me? Against me? No way of knowing.

"I'm going to concentrate on him alone. The Post-Impressionists can wait."

I smiled at this last sentence which, taken out of context, captured all the agonies of Van Gogh. It gave me an opportunity to ask him about something that had intrigued me since our first conversation.

"What about you . . . did you like painting before you joined the police or was it the other way around? I mean . . . how did this specializing come about?"

After a long silence he turned back towards me, still very calm, a little absent.

"You don't end up in this office by chance."

I looked around the desk and on the walls for some sort of clue. And I found nothing, not even a poster.

"You must keep abreast of what's going on in Paris, don't you?"

"I don't have time, I miss all the exhibitions I want to see. . . Before joining the force I wanted to. . . In 1972 I went to see a Francis Bacon exhibition. . . I was already a policeman. . . Do you know Bacon? Apparently he got the urge to paint almost by chance, when he saw some Picassos . . ."

And the chain stopped there, I thought.

"It must be a good job."

"Sometimes it is, but the bulk of it is people handling stolen goods, fakes, thefts . . . well, you see the sort of thing."

"You must see some amazing stuff, don't you?"

As I said that I realized I asked exactly the same

question of taxi drivers, anything to avoid talking about the weather.

"Yeah ... sometimes... There are nutters every-where but, in the arts, you could say we get our fair share."

If I ask for any details, he'll cut me dead, switch us back into our proper roles.

"Once I tailed an incredible guy, he specialized in Picasso, and his only distinguishing feature was that he had the *Demoiselles d'Avignon* tattooed at the top of his shoulder. Can you imagine checking that out on suspects when you're making discreet enquiries? Not long ago we cornered a Rembrandt in the Métro. Yes, a Rembrandt, rolled up in a tube of cardboard. Not listed anywhere. We don't get things like that every day... Right, well, I'm going to keep a very close eye on all this and I'd like it if we stayed in touch, I may need you. There may be no connection between your business and Monsieur Daufin's death, but I don't really believe that. I won't keep you any longer."

"Who can I get in touch with to see how Véro is getting on?"

"Baujon Hospital, but no one can see her at the moment. She'll stay there for a few days, I think. You can never really tell with nervous breakdowns."

I left his office feeling a bit stunned and, rather stupidly, I thanked him.

Delmas treated me like a normal person, not like a victim, and it made a change from the well-meaning embarrassment I've been treated to since my accident. It proves that the world doesn't stop at the end of my right wrist.

*

I have finished a bottle of over-chilled, slightly acrid Chablis and gone back to my table where my booty of crumpled paper is spread out. There isn't much there, actually, but it's all good. The Young Painters' Exhibition was put on in March, and the press cuttings include a few articles about the general tendencies but three of them report the unscheduled intervention made by four uncontrollable and completely uninhibited individuals on the twenty-seventh. The most interesting piece is from the June issue of a rag called *Art Libre* which no longer exists . . . and more's the pity.

[. . .] And then, amid a general purring which seemed to be the sum total of the Parisian response to the fine arts, we saw a note of dissent. Four young men burst into the gallery at the end of the evening. Just as masters and pupils were succumbing to the plaudits, this foursome hurled stones into the swamp of consensus and respectability. They shouted, calling for death to galleries and to their guard dogs, the "minor patrons of the arts". They took down paintings so that they could exhibit their own, they handed out leaflets and were extremely rude about the exhibitors [. . .]

Another review reproduced the text in the leaflet.

Since art is dead, let's give it a proper funeral!

We, the Objectivists, proclaim that art was killed by business interests, gallery owners, critics and other legitimizing bodies.

The Objectivists won't be cutting a single ear off.

It's too late.

The Objectivists will never make any claims, they do not exist, they will NEVER speculate about the names of any of their members. People don't sign corpses.

The Young Painters' Exhibition is just a hospice for aesthetics.

The Fine Arts are being assassinated.

And a good thing too.

In the third there is an account of the end of the evening. Some are scandalized, others acutely interested.

One of the exhibitors, feeling he had been insulted more than the others, tried to inform the police, but the organizers succeeded in quelling the climate of violence which was becoming a serious threat to their exhibition. By contrast, Edgar Delarge, owner of the Europe Gallery and famous for his pursuit of new talent – although some would say he confuses talent with mockery – announced that he was interested (!) in the young pseudo-revolutionaries. The four individuals, whose only merit was to remain true to the stance they had adopted, shouted him down for his "noxious trading in manure on canvas". (sic).

I so needed them to have existed.

The four of them had succeeded in creating this mayhem. Chemin may be losing his teeth, but his memory is still reliable. It's all there: the cradle of the Fine Arts, the rebellion, the spitting in the face of business interests, the contempt for appointed officials, the anonymity and the refusal to acknowledge their own work. Morand was there before becoming Morand.

And then there was this gallery owner, Delarge, an "entrepreneur" like the others, but this one had the enterprise to "declare his interest". You really had to be mad, or to love a bit of scandal, or to love the Objectivists to stand up to their insolence. That's where I can carry on my research because, in its own quiet way, their assault of 27 June bore some fruit . . . even if it only amounted to influencing the acquisitions committee. And why couldn't they have broken with their great claim of integrity a second time? Surely Delarge must remember, he could tell me about his confrontation with them, or even describe it physically, he may have seen their studio or kept an eye on the rest of their output. At least he could tell me what it was about these young terrorists that he liked so much. And as I turn to look at *Attempt 30* for the thousandth time, I feel I would like someone else – someone more informed and impassioned – to explain in simple words what it is that I feel. Chemin could have been that person but he lost his eye long ago, somewhere in a chromo of the Everglades. And I need to know everything because behind this painting there is a lunatic, a twisted mind who crushes memories, cuts off hands and caves in skulls. A gentleman with a Stanley knife. A madman who talks in the dark. And I'll find him before Delmas.

*

Probably to prove to myself that I was still capable of feelings for other human beings and particularly to try and tighten the connections that belong only to me with people who belong only to me, I went back to the typewriter. I felt inspired to use a style that would translate a soft, pastel-coloured languor without losing sight of a good grasp of realism. Impressionism, to be precise.

Dear you two
  I've hardly ever written to you and fate has dictated that, now that I'm taking the trouble to, I can only do it with one hand. I'm travelling through difficult uncharted waters, and you, despite the distance between us, are my only landmarks. I'll have to let more time go by before I can see more clearly. I miss the sun and the sea that you have never tried to leave behind.

*

A man's voice.

"Europe Gallery, good morning."

"I would like to speak to Monsieur Delarge."

"Can I ask you what it's concerning?"

"An interview."

". . . Are you a journalist? Is this to do with the Pompidou Centre?"

"No, not at all, I'm trying to get information about the Young Painters' Exhibition in 1964, and I think he was there. Could I speak to him please?"

A subtle feeling of hesitation. If he hadn't been there they would have told me straightaway. I even wonder whether . . .

". . . Um . . . he only speaks to people by prior appointment, but he's very busy at the moment. What exactly would you like to know . . . ?"

I sensed the defensive reflex. No doubt about it, he can talk about him in the third person all he likes . . .

"It's not easy to get things across on the telephone. Could I make an appointment and come to the gallery?"

"You won't find him here. What do you want to know about the Young Painters' Exhibition?"

"It would be easier if I just came over."

"Not at the moment! What's your name?"

"I'll call back later."

I hung up before he had time to turn me down a third time. I thought it would be a good manoeuvre calling first but I cocked up. I can't always see my tactical errors coming. All I can do now is dash over there straightaway to pluck him while he's still warm, before he has time to run for it. His gallery is in the Marais area, on the Rue Barbette, not far from my apartment. I know it's crazy but artistic tendencies are gaining ground in my part of Paris. The Pompidou Centre has spawned some offspring.

I'm there in less than five minutes, and he hasn't been able to get away in the meantime. There is only one nameplate at number 59: "Europe Gallery". You have to go through the porch to get to the exhibition rooms. In the courtyard surrounded by old buildings you are hit full in the face by the pale, pale blue of the two floors next to entrance C. The gallery doorway is magnificently designed with a pair of doors in glass and metal, weighing over a thousand pounds each, but you barely have to touch them to open them. Inside, hardly anything. That's the fashion. Empty space is hugely important, the original stonework is kept, stripped but impeccably restored, the floor is elephant grey, like the Hall of Mirrors at Versailles, a skating rink. And in the distance there are actually a few elegantly hung paintings. The reception desk is recessed into a wall so as not to interrupt the sightlines. I feel utterly alone on an island of modernity. A badly dressed, Baroque castaway in an ocean of Minimalism. I leaf through the visitors' book and recognize a few signatures, the same ones as at the Coste Gallery, the indigenous fauna of private views. Beside it is the list of the Delarge stable, his catalogue of artists, and – as I run through the list of his protégés, his foals – I get a clearer idea of why he doesn't need to make a song and dance. His collection brings together at least four or five of the most sought-after artists of the day. It's clear that this man has better things to do than waste time on people like me ferreting around. And when you have people like Lasewitz, Béranger and Linnel in your stable (to name only the ones that mean something to me), you call the shots on price. I've already hung a Lasewitz, a series of overlapping empty frames to suggest a labyrinth. Ten minutes to hang them, three hours to work out which order to put them in ... Béranger makes luminous boxes, he photographs his feet, his nose or his chubby belly, he has them blown up to giant size and then lights them up in boxes stuffed with fluorescent bulbs. The photo goes from just five ounces to 260 pounds, and it takes six men with straps to put it in position. Linnel's name also means something to me, but I'm not really sure what he does. On spec I would say he's one of the rare few who still uses paints and a brush.

"Can I help you?"

She emerged from behind three pillars of breezeblocks that act as a passage through to a side office. A very pretty young woman with strawberry blond hair and blue eyes. She's not the ideal build for turning away the unwashed.

"I would like to meet Monsieur Delarge."

She tidies a few files on the desk, just to have something to do with her hands.

"Do you have an appointment?"

"No, but I could make one right away."

"That won't be possible at the moment, he's setting up an exhibition, he's right in the middle of hanging it."

Try another one. . . I look behind the breezeblocks, never doubting for a moment that Delarge is hiding there. With this system of slightly bevelled pillars they can keep an eye on comings and goings in the gallery without having to spend their time in it if there's no one there.

Delarge saw me come in. I can feel him there, not far away, skulking. What's he got to be afraid of? Was I too direct? Maybe I shouldn't have mentioned 1964. Am I scared? This need for tactics is becoming a pain, it's impossible to get any information without triggering a whole process of suspicion. And I'm starting to get caught up in the paranoid fear of too much said and not enough said.

"Come back in a fortnight, and ring first. He might have a moment."

Ring? No thanks. I'm not giving warnings any more.

"What sort of exhibition is it at the Pompidou Centre?"

"Linnel, one of our artists. From April eighth to the thirtieth."

"Three weeks? What a triumph. . . Not everyone gets to the Pompidou Centre . . ."

As I speak I can clearly picture the sign I saw at the Pompidou Centre yesterday saying "New exhibition coming soon", and the picture-hangers in a quandary.

With a satisfied little twist to her lip, she utters an: "oh no . . .!"

It's true. For a living artist, it's the Holy Grail. After the Pompidou Centre all there is left to hope for is the Louvre, a few centuries later.

"Leave your name and contact details in the visitors' book, I'll let him know you came by . . ."

She hands me the pen, and I can't help thinking she knows she's being devious.

"I never sign visitors' books."

She throws the pen down on the table with obvious contempt.

"It's your loss . . ."

"On the other hand, I'd very much like an invitation to the private view at the Pompidou Centre. It is by invitation only, isn't it?"

"No, I'm so sorry, I've given them all out . . ."

"Are these works by Linnel?"

She bursts out laughing. I don't understand why, and I find it irritating.

"They are part of Monsieur Delarge's private collection. He likes to display them to the public from time to time instead of locking them away in a safe. They're made to be seen, wouldn't you say?"

If I'd read the signatures instead of asking inane questions. . . There was plenty there to laugh about: a small Kandinsky, a Braque collage and I don't know the third, but that's probably hardly surprising for someone who can't identify the first two.

*

I don't really have any choice. This private view at the Pompidou Centre is the day after tomorrow in the evening, and I can't really hope to corner Delarge before then. Or even afterwards, he'll find some masterly way to avoid me if that's what he wants. Something's worrying him and – to find out what – I have to ask him face to face, that's all there is to it. He's succeeded in getting one of his foals into the Pompidou Centre and that's more than just a victory for a dealer, it's a crowning moment. Not to mention the manna, the stacks of money it will bring in for him. He'll be there right from the beginning, at this private view, given that he's the one who's doing the inviting. There will be plenty of chat about prices, there will be dozens of potential buyers, those who already have and those who don't yet have "Linnels" in their collections. All the right people will be there with their chit-chat and their glasses of champagne . . . and me in the middle of it all. Delarge won't be able to get rid of me in front of so many people.

"Hello, Liliane?"

". . . . Antoine . . . hey . . . how are you?"

"Is Coste at the gallery?"

"No."

"I need an invite to the Linnel exhibition the day after tomorrow."

"We got it a couple of days ago, but it's for . . ."

"For the boss, I know. And I want it. I want it. I really want it. You'll just have to say it was delayed in the post. Has she seen it yet?"

"No, but . . . you're a pain, Antoine."

"She'll get in anyway, the mighty Coste isn't the sort who gets held up at the door to the Pompidou Centre."

"You disappear, we don't hear a word about you, then you call when you need something."

"I need it."

"Will you come and pick it up?"

"Will you send it to me?"

"You really are a prick."

"Big kiss . . . and it's a long time since I've kissed anyone . . ."

*

Two days of waiting. No, not even that. Of backing off. Living in fear that I might get a call from Delmas to tell me something major has happened, that there's been serious progress in his enquiries. Nothing could be worse for me. I haven't been out much. For about an hour I thought I might be able to go back to the academy, convinced that I owed them all an explanation: Angelo, René, Benoît and the others. But I haven't dared to.

It's five o'clock on Tuesday, and I've just come back from my neighbour who has tied my tie. I thought my usual clothes would be a bit out of place at the private view. At that sort of reception people don't chat so readily to a tramp, even I would be wary of some bloke in a jacket gaping halfway down his thighs to reveal shapeless green cords. This time I've made a bit of an effort and taken out the panoply of outfits I had for private views at the Coste. I've shaved with a real blade, I felt like it, and I didn't cut myself once.

The entrance is on the Rue du Renard to avoid all the bustle on the pedestrianized square. I show my invitation to two men in blue who wish me a pleasant evening. I think back to all those private views I escaped from at the Coste, not even getting a taste of that satisfaction which comes from a job well done. Jacques would be hurt if he could see me now, with a tie on. A sort of hostess hands me a press pack and points out the stairs that lead up to the exhibition. Upstairs there are thirty or so people, some of whom are already in full flow with their commentaries, as if they have already done the rounds of the walls. That makes sense; the people who come to private views aren't there to see paintings, because it's almost impossible to see an exhibition in all that commotion with figures obstructing the line of vision and empty champagne glasses on the edges of the ashtrays.

While waiting for the festivities to kick off, I go for a bit of a wander round the show, not to see what Linnel does, no I don't really care about that. But just to admire – or even criticize – the picture-hanger's work.

Canvasses six and a half feet by five, oils. White gloves compulsory. Nice work, except for one piece, which should have been about eight inches higher because of the plinth which is a bit too obtrusive. And there's another one, a smaller one, which could have done with being at eye level. In one of the rooms I get the feeling the lighting was done in a bit of a hurry, a spotlight casting a nasty shadow over a sizeable area of canvas. Other sorry but inevitable details: the hopeless efforts to camouflage fire extinguishers. No colour in the world can rival the bright red of those delicate instruments; it's every gallery-owner's downfall. The cards with the titles and dates are nailed too close to the paintings; Jacques always managed to forget them. Apart from that, nothing to say, nice exhibition. It would have taken my colleague and myself three days, tops. We preferred the tricky things, where there was some twist to every piece, glass balls balancing on a point, mobiles suspended without any visible means of support, bicycle chains in perpetual motion, frescoes with strange optical effects, anything fragile, breakable, cryptic, wacky, funny and – in a word – unhangable.

The bar is open, I can tell from the subtle ebb of people instigated by it. I insinuate my way into the wave. In the room where the buffet is laid out it's all noise. A concert of chatter punctuated by interjections and discreet laughter. A few familiar faces, critics, some less prudish painters, an official from the Ministry. I revolve very slowly on the spot as I activate my sonar. And a few feet from the dense cluster of people around the glasses, I pick up a definite beep-beep. Looking through the press pack I come across a photo taken at the Biennale in Sao Paulo, a row of artists posing as if for a class photo with Delarge standing to the right in pride of place, like the teacher. He is here, in the flesh, a few feet away, with two other men a little younger than himself. Linnel is on his right. He's playing his part as the artist at his own private view: shaking the hands proffered to him, thanking sundry enthusiasms without worrying about their sincerity quotient. An artist in the place of honour can choose not to smile and not to say anything, it's one of his few privileges. He does, however, have to agree to meet journalists, but would rather avoid buyers – there are other people for that. Alain Linnel seems to be playing the game, limply, a bit serious, a bit affected, a bit absent. A waiter brings them some glasses, I move closer and position myself a couple of feet or so from them, with my back turned to them and my ears wide open, pretending to squeeze through to the buffet.

I'm in luck. I very quickly understand the situation, I haven't cocked up, the oldest one is Delarge and he's introducing his prodigy to an art critic, one Alex Ramey. Definitely one of the most feared in all Paris, the only one who can ruin an exhibition with a couple of adjectives. I remember one of his reviews about an exhibition at the Coste; the piece was so incendiary that a good smattering of visitors came just to confirm the extent of the disaster.

But the critic likes what he sees this evening, and he obviously wants to tell the artist himself and, before long, his readers.

"Would tomorrow suit you for an interview?"

A slight hesitation, nothing is forthcoming. Delarge, overflowing with goodwill and still radiant, urges him gently.

"Come on, Alain! You must have a few minutes tomorrow . . ."

Still nothing. Not even a stammer. I turn round to cast an eye over this situation that seems, to say the least, a little tense. And it is then that I realize I too have got something slightly wrong.

"No. I won't find a few minutes for this man."

Bang. Hadn't foreseen that one. I crane my head trying to imagine the sort of expression a dealer like Delarge might be wearing as he grapples with a capricious artist taking the luxury of refusing to give an interview the very day after a private view.

"You're joking, Alain . . ."

"Not at all. I won't answer questions from someone who referred to me as a 'decorator' four or five years ago. Do you remember, Monsieur Ramey? It was a little exhibition at the old gallery on the Ile Saint-Louis. And you remember it too, dear Edgar, don't pretend you've forgotten everything now that I'm at the Pompidou Centre. At the time you said he was a bastard, don't try to deny it . . ."

I must be dreaming!

I can feel the weight of all this going on behind my back. I make the most of a little gap in the herd of drinkers to grab a brimming glass. Which I down in three gulps. Ramey is still there.

"Listen, don't put criticism on trial for me, we all know the routine. . . Your painting has evolved and so has the way people look at it."

"It's true, Alain . . . we shouldn't get all touchy about this," Delarge goes on.

"What do you mean 'we'? You've always said 'we' when you mean 'you'. This man could drag me through the shit tomorrow morning, he could drag 'us' through the shit. I think I'd rather like it. On that note, I'm going to get myself another drink."

Consternation. Delarge takes Ramey off by the arm and launches into an explosion of apologies. I grab another glass and drink it down in one. Never heard anything like it. . . I don't know whether I'm feeling a cynical jubilation or a vague uneasiness, because – after

101

a blow like that – Delarge won't tolerate the tiniest question from a pain in the arse like me. The hubbub is intensifying, the champagne still flowing, and the crowd becoming noticeably more of a crush. Linnel is shaking other hands and laughing quite genuinely; he doesn't only have enemies. I don't let him out of my sight. A slightly paunchy man taps him on the shoulder and he turns round, shakes his hand and goes back to his conversation without really worrying about the new arrival who he's left standing there like a lemon. And I know that face, as everyone does, apparently. A painter? A critic? An inspector? I want to know and, with no feeling of embarrassment, I ask the woman next to me whether she knows him. Very relaxed and already slightly drunk, she answers as if I've just landed from another galaxy:

"That's Reinhard. . . Have you seen any sweet canapés doing the rounds?"

"Reinhard . . . the auctioneer?"

"Of course! With Dalloyau, I always like the sweet stuff."

"Listen, I can see a tray, over to the left. If you can reach me some of those little salmon things for me, we could do a trade."

She smiles, we do the swap and she orders two more glasses of champagne to wash it all down.

"Lovely exhibition," she says.

"I wouldn't know," I say with my mouth full.

She bursts out laughing. My right sleeve is tucked well into my pocket. Among all these society people it might look like a rather snobbish pose. A particular type. She feverishly puts away a succession of coffee-flavoured mini éclairs, and I take the opportunity to slip away. Reinhard is talking to Delarge, who's still fuming. This time, I describe a parabola round the

102

room to end up in front of the painting closest to them. I remember a conversation with Coste about Reinhard's lineage, auctioneers from father to son for as long as the profession has existed. He authenticates, values and sells a good share of everything that goes through the salerooms at Drouot. What a job that is: striking a hammer at ten thousand francs a go . . . enough to give Jacques his doubts, him and his whole toolbox.

Delarge is irritated and speaking in a half whisper; I can only get half of what he's saying.

"He pisses me off, you know. . . I've been preparing for this exhibition for two years . . . and the government commission with all the shit we're in . . .!"

Reinhard grumbles something inaudible.

Right, let's recap: Delarge has got problems with one of the foals from his stable who seems a bit quick to buck and rear. Reinhard, who's another thoroughbred but on a different racecourse, is in on the secret. All these people are in a mess, and none of that is going to get my cause ahead by so much as one length. I'll have to drum up the resolve to corner the dealer before his private view falls apart, get him to cough up what he can and go home. The champagne's gone to my head a bit, and it won't be long before I run out of patience. Reinhard is moving away towards Linnel, this is my only opportunity to take on Delarge. I pat his upper arm, he turns round and takes a slight step back. Oddly enough, the alcohol has made the job easier for me.

"You don't know me, and I won't bother you for long. I tried to get hold of you at the gallery to talk to you about something which dates back to 1964. The Young Painters' Exhibition. I read in the press cuttings that you were there, and I wanted to know . . ."

He looks away, his cheeks are flushing like a child's and his hands are shaking like an old man's. He's already wished I would go and roast in hell a hundred times.

"I can't . . . there are lots of people I need to see . . . I . . ."

"You spoke to a group, there were four of them, 'The Objectivists'. You took an interest in their work. I just wanted to know what you remember of them, try to think . . ."

". . . The who? . . . '64 is a long time ago. . . Maybe . . . twenty-five years ago. . . I was just starting out. . . The journalist must have got it wrong. . . Anyway, I never went to the Young Painters' Exhibition, or even to the Paris Biennale. . . I can't be of any use to you . . ."

I hold him back by his sleeve but he pulls away and makes off without another word. He goes back towards Linnel and Reinhard. They've stopped staring at me now that I'm looking at them. Only Linnel has kept his eyes riveted on me and is staring me up and down. . . I have a horrible feeling his gaze is stopping at the end of my right arm, buried in my pocket. Is he sniggering? Perhaps. . . I don't know where to look any more, my lower arm is gripped with cramp, but now I know that somewhere, in all this crush, there is what Delmas would call a "seat of presumption".

All of a sudden I feel small, disabled and afraid of losing the thing that gave me strength – the pleasure of eradicating a culprit. All these people are beyond me, bigger than me, nothing here belongs to me, not the paintings or the ties, not the complicated words or the champagne, not the sound of all that pontificating, the perfumed sweatiness or the limp handshakes, and not the agonies of art and its obscure conflicts. I was made for the dust that comes off the baize, for silence skimming over ivory, for balls colliding sweetly and Angelo's exaltation, for the smell of cigars and old men in braces, for blue chalk and that permanent gleam of serenity deep in my own eyes. And it's to get that back some day, perhaps, that I have to stay a little longer in all this absurd circus.

Someone jogs me, and I don't even have time to complain before the girl has carried on, heading straight for Delarge and coming to stand squarely in front of him. From the front I wouldn't know, but from behind you can make out a fierce determination. She's talking loudly, and the three men have now completely forgotten me. Perfect diversion. Delarge's face goes to pieces again. Not a good evening. This thought is rather comforting and gives me my second wind. Linnel bursts out laughing so loudly that, this time, the conversations around them stop. I go over towards the buffet again to listen, like everyone else there.

"I'm not interested in your private view, Monsieur Delarge, but this seems to be the only way to see you face to face!"

Excuse me? How many of us are there exactly in the same situation?

"Please, mademoiselle, is this the time to come and make a scandal?" Delarge says, his cheeks burning.

"Scandal? Who are you to talk about scandal? My paper will publish a whole dossier on your fraud!"

"Be careful what you insinuate, mademoiselle."

"I'm not insinuating anything, I'm shouting out loud for everyone to hear!"

Barking mad and furious, she has cupped her hands round her mouth and started shouting to the room at large.

"Anyone here who's bought work by the famous Cubist Juan Alfonso can start worrying now!"

"Quite right too!" adds Linnel, bent over laughing.

Delarge throws him a filthy look and pushes the girl away, waving at the two henchmen on the door, who materialize instantly beside him.

"This woman's mad, my lawyer will take care of all this! Get her out of here!"

The two men almost pick her up and drag her towards the door. Now I don't know if I'm dreaming or witnessing a brilliantly staged event. She's struggling and still going on with her infernal incantations.

"The truth about Juan Alfonso, in the May issue of *Artefact*! On sale everywhere!"

The crowd has frozen, for one everlasting moment. The silent, gaping mouths no longer close, the glasses stay poised against lips, and arms held up in the air – stiff with surprise – no longer come back down. A Hieronymous Bosch panel, in three dimensions.

The only one who still knows how to talk is Linnel.

"Wonderful. . . Wonderful. . . This is wonderful . . ."

It doesn't look as if his provocation is going down too well. Especially with Delarge, who clearly has an overwhelming urge to thump him and tell him how ungrateful he is. A new wave of people draws gently towards the buffet. Someone automatically hands me a glass, probably because the general consensus is that everyone needs one. A scandal . . . And, seen from where I'm standing, a wonderful episode, as Linnel says. Delarge seems to have more than one dodgy scandal in his wake. Never heard of the Cubist whose name I've already forgotten, or of the nefarious goings-on around him. I adopt a degree of compassion for this man, this art dealer who should have triumphed this evening and who's done nothing but suffer attacks from the press, from his own artist and from snoopers like me. I should have stayed for private views more often.

People are gradually picking up their conversations again. There are trays of canapés back on the tables.

"That girl was wonderful, wasn't she? I mean, turning the Pompidou Centre into a Grévin museum, not bad . . ."

The words just slipped into my ear, and I swivel round.

Linnel, smiling from ear to ear.

The man must be a bit touched in the head.

"Yes. . . It came over as a bit of a publicity stunt, didn't it? A funny publicity stunt, but still," I say.

"Perhaps, but I really like rude people. You get so bored in scrums like this. And then . . . I'm here because I have to be – I'm the one who did all this stuff that's hanging on the walls – but what about the others?"

"The others? They like this sort of thing, that's all."

"What about you, do you like it?"

"I dunno. If I had to say something, it would be a bit rude."

He laughs and so do I but my laugh gets strangled in my throat when he slips his arm under mine. My bad one.

"Come with me, I'll give you a little personal tour."

Before setting off round the rooms, he fills two glasses and hands me one, and I just stand there like a prick, stuck between the glass being offered to me and the stranger's hand parked against my ribs.

He gets me to clink glasses, and I obey but slightly lose my balance. He stops me in front of a painting.

"Look at this one, it's an old one, from '71."

I don't know what he wants from me, whether this

is a carefully thought out manoeuvre or the latest escapade of a drunken artist. Either way, he knows that I've caused his dealer some grief, and perhaps that's what he likes. In fact, it's the first time I've had a look at his work; I went too quickly earlier and I didn't see a thing. I always tend to like the frames more than what's in them. Long brushstrokes of a rather dirty green, you get the feeling each stream of colour was painted in a straight line, then diverted towards the end. Then he covered the whole thing with white, taking over the entire surface. I don't really know what to think of it. It's totally abstract. That's all.

"Does it do anything for you?"

"Something, yes. . . You know, I don't know anything about it . . ."

"Good, specialists wind me up. And I'd really like someone like you to tell me what they think this evening. So, what does it say to you?"

"You should talk to someone else. I only go by the response from my retina – primal and reactionary. That's what everyone says when they're scared to commit, and I'm one of them. The bottom line is I can't tell between a good painting and a bad one. Can you give me a tip?"

"Yes, it's simple, you just have to have seen a few thousand of them already, that's all. So, what does it say to you?"

"Pff. . . If I really think. . . It might make me think of a mother sheltering her daughter under her coat because it's raining."

Curious silence.

I said it so earnestly that he isn't even laughing. It just came to me on impulse.

"Right, okay, everyone sees what they want in it. I wasn't thinking of that when I did it but . . . well. . . I can't say anything. And do you know how much it costs?"

"If you're someone who gets exhibited at the Pompidou Centre, it must cost a bomb."

"More than that. This one's 125,000. One night's work, if I remember right."

Misfire. It doesn't impress me. I once saw a pile of empty beer cans come into the gallery, and they were worth twice that.

"And how much for the dealer?"

"Too much. The rule's fifty-fifty, but we have a special arrangement."

"And you work at night?"

"Oh yes, and I'm one of the only painters in the world who likes artificial light. That way I have a surprise at dawn . . ."

He hails a passing waiter in a white jacket, and the man comes back a minute later with some champagne. He wants to clink glasses again. A couple comes over towards us, the woman kisses Linnel, and the man does the same. The artist proffers his cheeks unenthusiastically.

"Oh, Alain, it's fantastic. Are you pleased? It's really powerful, you can feel a buzz, do you know what I mean, the pieces create such a dialogue, it's excellent."

He thanks them as if he has a clothes peg on his nose and drags me somewhere else. The man's mad.

"What does 'the pieces create a dialogue' mean?" I ask.

I actually know better than anyone, it's the expression Coste used to use. But I just wanted to get him to talk.

"Nothing. If we started listening to that sort of crap . . ."

"Still. . . I find that impressive, these people who speak in code. Without it, you can't get anywhere."

"Really? I hate every kind of jargon. André Breton used to say 'any philosopher I don't understand is a bastard!' I quite often laugh till I cry when I read the learned articles about my daubings. You know, contemporary painting lends itself to that sort of thing much better than, say, music. What on earth could you say about music, hey? Art critics don't talk about what they see; they just try to be even more abstract than the canvases. They even admit it themselves."

I've read a shed-load of those incomprehensible catalogues.

"Still . . . it's impressive."

"Right, nothing could be easier, we can wander gently between the guests and I'll do a simultaneous translation for you, okay?"

The champagne makes me laugh mischievously. My brain must be starting to look a bit like an emulsion of brut impérial.

"Okay."

I may well be inebriated but I'm not forgetting a thing . . . not Delarge or my stump. Whatever he may have in mind, Linnel could be a useful joker to have in my pack.

Without looking for anyone in particular we come within earshot of two slightly ageing women, one of whom is on particularly eloquent form. The smoke from a cigarette in the corner of her mouth is keeping her left eye closed.

"You know, Linnel often plays on chromatic equivalences, but still . . . there's that need for implosion . . ."

Linnel's aside:

"What she means is I always use the same colours,

and 'implosion' means you have to look at the pictures for a long time before anything happens."

The old dear goes on:

"You get a strong sense of the matt qualities of the surface . . . then there's something emerging, here . . . breaking through the veil . . ."

Linnel:

"She's saying off-white's a bland colour and you can see what's behind it."

It seems to me the exhibition rooms are getting fuller and fuller. The two old girls move away, but others take their place, a couple in which the woman doesn't dare say a thing until the bloke has spoken. He hesitates as if absolutely compelled to express an opinion.

"It's. . . It's interesting," he says.

Linnel turns to me with a nasty glint in his eye.

"With him it's not complicated, he just wants to say it's rubbish."

I laugh again, quite openly this time. He has a way about him that I really like, he's the disillusioned artist who couldn't give a damn about the decorum and the pretentious song and dance that revolves around anything set up as dogma. Anything except for what he does, on his own, at home. His daubing. The sacred thing he doesn't talk about. Those moments I myself have experienced when you feel you are the author, the actor and the only spectator.

"Hey, let's go and get shit-faced," he asks me, absolutely seriously.

"Let's do that!" I've answered without even realizing it.

I do wonder where he picked up that vocabulary, it's like listening to René. Could Linnel be the prodigal working-class son who first started painting in wood primer, doing landscapes of suburban wastelands and still-lifes of buggered mopeds? I don't know if it's the champagne or the bloke's gentle irony, but I'm feeling much better than when I arrived.

We clink glasses.

"Has your dealer got a government commission on his back? I know I'm prying . . ."

"Prying? You're joking . . . it's in all the papers, a bitch of a fresco that'll cover a whole wall of the Ministry building. And it's not him who's got a government commission on his back, it's me."

I give a long, loud whistle.

". . . You? Well, this must be the year of the Linnel! The Pompidou Centre and a government commission! What a triumph! What luck!"

"Yeah, really, 300 square feet . . . and I don't have a clue what to put up there for them. . . They want to inaugurate it next year."

"Have you started on it?"

"Yes and no. . . I've got a vague idea. . . It's going to be called 'Hoodathawt', a 250-foot dick coming out of the building, all in pinks and purples. What do you think the Minister will make of me then?"

For a moment I thought he was serious. Delarge has got plenty to worry about with a nutter like him. I think I have a better understanding of what is going on, the poor dealer is dependent on an artist who is quite capable of going off on one at the height of his success. His six-foot by three-foot paintings are already over-priced, so I dread to think how much the fresco's costing.

"I'm going to find something to drink, will you wait for me?"

I nod. Someone's just smacked a deafening "Hello!" into my left ear.

Coste.

"I'm a bit late because they were so awkward on the door, I've lost my invitation. . . How are you? I didn't know you came to private views at the Pompidou Centre. Do you know Linnel? I mean . . . do you know him personally?"

She must have seen me drinking with him. And that would intrigue Coste, seeing the ex-hanger from her gallery knocking back drinks with an artist from the Pompidou Centre.

"I didn't even know him by name before getting here. And do you like his paintings?" I ask her before she has a chance to ask me.

"Yes, very much. I've been following his work for four or five years and I've . . ."

I'm drunk, I'm going to have to face up to it. And, therefore, short on patience. I wait for her to finish her sentence so that I can set off on another subject. Old Mother Coste is a living encyclopaedia, and I mustn't miss this opportunity.

"Do you know Juan Alfonso?"

She frowns at me, surprised by the change of subject.

". . . Um. . . Yes, vaguely, but I don't know much about him. . . He's a Cubist no one had really heard of until very recently. A hundred and fifty of his pieces were sold at Drouot, that's all I know. Are you interested in Cubism?"

"No."

"When are you going to come back and work for us?"

"I've got one or two things to sort out first, then I'll see."

"Have you heard about what happened at the depot?"

"Yes, I saw Superintendent Delmas."

Linnel comes back with a bottle and shakes Coste's hand. They exchange a few quick niceties, and she heads off towards the other rooms, apologizing for having not yet seen the exhibition.

"You see that woman there," says Linnel, "she's one of the few really sincere people in this business. She didn't wait till I got here before liking my stuff."

I'm happy to hear him say that. I'd always suspected that my ex-boss really did like what she does.

"Right, that's enough of that bollocks, we've got behind, pour us a drink!" he says, handing me a glass and a bottle.

"I can't. . . I'd rather you poured . . ."

To clarify the situation, I take my sleeve from my pocket and show him the stump. In spite of myself, this gesture has become the finishing blow to my dialectics.

"Well that's not very handy!"

Delarge is taking his protégé by the shoulders. It's too late.

"Alain, we need you for some photos, please excuse us," he says to me with a smile which makes Judas's kiss look like a touch of tenderness.

"I haven't got time, Edgar, can't you see I'm chatting to my friend? And my friend is an enlightened art-lover! He really genuinely is!"

Delarge bites his lip.

"Stop it, Alain . . . ST-O-O-O-P . . . you're going too far."

"Go and look after your guests, you've always been better at that than me . . ."

"Your . . . friend can cope without you for a minute. And it will stop him asking too many questions."

In my clouded mind I felt that was one sentence too many. The exhibition rooms seemed empty, I hadn't noticed the time passing. I closed my eyes and saw a few shapeless black clouds scudding across my eyelids. I raised my arms slowly and my fist completed its

114

arabesque smack in the middle of Delarge's face. It had to come out. I grabbed him by the collar to head-butt him two or three times, his nose shattered but my screaming masked his, then I kneed him and kicked him, shaking off the anger that had been accumulating for too long. He fell, not me, and I felt that made things more convenient: I aimed for his head with the tip of my shoe, just one last, definitive . . .

Didn't have time, two blokes got me away from him right at that moment, and I howled because I hadn't satisfied that urge. The one closest to me took the blow, in the tibia, he bent over; the other one grabbed hold of me and slammed me to the floor, my stump slipped and my face crashed down onto the carpet. A punch in the back of my neck crushed it a bit further. I was snatched up by my hair and forced to get up.

Someone mentioned the police.

Over in a corner I saw Linnel pouring himself a drink.

Delarge, who was still on the floor, bellowed an order.

To chuck me out.

The two men, who had been watching the door, took an arm each, twisted them round behind my back and dragged me all the way to the Rue du Renard. One of them, in a last spasm of violence, yanked at my hair to jerk my head round.

I saw a great strip of night sky before taking the side of his hand full in the face.

*

I waited a long time, I've lost track, a good twenty minutes, before a heroic taxi driver stopped beside this wreck in a tie sitting with his head among the

115

stars waiting for his nose to be good enough to stop bleeding. Before opening the door he handed me a box of tissues.

"Shall we go to a chemist?"

"Not worth it."

"Where then?"

I've already been thinking about that as I've sobered up, lying on the ventilation grill above Rambuteau station. In the little sleeve for my travel pass I found the address of the only man I know who would really be able to dress a wound. My nose is hurting and I'll only entrust it to a doctor. Right now, I really hope he isn't married.

"Rue de la Fontaine-au-Roi."

"We're off."

I throw away the sticky red mass that can't absorb any more blood and tear off another handful of tissues.

"I'm being careful with your upholstery," I say.

"Oh, I'm not fussed, if it had been puke I wouldn't have taken you. I can't stand vomit."

The whole way there he didn't try to find out why my nose was pissing blood, and he left me on the doorstep to number 32. I appreciated the quality of his silence.

Briançon, fourth floor, left. The stairwell smells of piss, and the light doesn't work. Through his door I can hear music playing softly, oboe, perhaps. I ring the bell.

"Antoine . . .?"

The red all down my shirtfront means I don't have to speak; I go in.

"But what. . .? Sit yourself down."

I keep my head tilted back and he sits me down,

116

then walks round the room for a bit before coming back with everything he needs to clean up my face.

A compress burns my nose.

"Is it broken?" I ask.

"If it were broken, you'd know."

"It's standing up well considering everything it's been subjected to this year . . ."

"Have you been in a fight?"

"Yes, and it felt good. You're right, Doctor, with a bit of determination you can overcome handicaps, I flattened two of them, just like that. As if I were all there. And when I was all there I never flattened anyone."

"Do you think you're being funny?"

While we waited for my nose to clot we sat in silence, for a good fifteen minutes. Then he took off my jacket and shirt and put a clean sweatshirt on me. I accepted everything, quite docile, everything except the drink.

"I've been waiting for you to come and see me," he said, "but under different circumstances."

"But I often think of you. I'm making progress."

"If you really want to make progress you'd do better to come and see me at Boucicaut. There are all sorts of physiotherapy equipment there. You'd only need three months."

"Never. It'll come of its own accord, it's like love. We've only just met, and right now, I'm only flirting shyly with my left side. Then we'll get to trusting and helping each other, and one day it'll be a firm, loyal couple. Takes time."

"Wasted time. Have you found a job?"

"A policeman's already asked me that."

He pauses deliberately.

"Has your attacker been found?"

"Not yet."

"And is there a connection with what happened this evening?"

For a moment I almost blurted it all out to him, in one go, to get it all into the open. If I hadn't had my face smashed in, I'm sure I would have spewed out all the bile inside me.

"None at all. I was drunk and I tested the patience of some people a bit stronger than me. But I wouldn't have missed it for anything in the world."

A long silence. The doctor is looking at me differently now and shaking his head gently.

"You take it too well, Antoine."

"Can I stay here?"

". . . Um. . . If you like. I've only got this sofa."

"Perfect."

Once he had found some sheets and a pillow for me we said goodnight to each other.

"Slam the door as you go out, I'm bound to leave before you do. Come and see me soon, and don't wait till you've got blood all over your face."

I didn't add anything to that. Once he had shut the door to his bedroom I was sure I would never see him again.

*

Sleep took a long time coming, and even then it didn't last long. I left at about five o'clock in the morning without even bothering to write a thank-you note to Briançon. I thought the night air would do me some good and that my nose needed to be in the cold. If I drag my feet, I can get back to the Marais in about half an hour by going up the Rue Oberkampf. Longer than I need to picture how I'm going to get through the coming day. The doctor's right, I'm feeling all right, almost calm, and I shouldn't be. I've already forgotten the punches: the ones I dealt and the ones I took. One day it will cost me my nose, but it won't have any more effect on me than this. A hand, a nose, mental health. In the state I'm in . . .

Delarge is a bastard, and Linnel is mad. But, given the choice, I did the right thing by thumping the first. And I'm pretty sure I'll have another go soon if he doesn't tell me what he knows about the Objectivists. That's the difference between Delmas and me. Delarge would always find some way to keep a policeman busy, with his lawyers and his connections. He would have to be seriously in the shit to feel worried. And all I've got to confront him with is my left hand. But it seems to be responding better and better.

I went up the stairs in a muck sweat, gasping for breath, with heavy legs. My arm isn't the only thing that has atrophied. On the corner of the desk I spotted a sheet of white paper rolled into the carriage of the typewriter, and I felt inspired. This time, after the absurd events I had just experienced, I felt like brutal disparate images. An arbitrary juxtaposition of elements that ultimately produce a meaningless violence. Surrealism.

Dear you two
From now on my life is as beautiful as the chance encounter between a glass of champagne and the stump of an arm on a burned canvas. Viva la muerte.

I lay down, just for a moment, but sleep crept up on me and I sank into oblivion.

While drinking a cup of coffee I looked through the

press pack the hostess had given me. Nothing very new, except for a little paragraph on the history of the relationship between the dealer and the artist. It's almost believable:

"Edgar Delarge first took an interest in Alain Linnel's work as early as 1967, and it was more than a discovery: it was a passion. He did everything he could to bring the young artist to the public eye. This is also the story of a long personal friendship. Alain Linnel has proved his loyalty too by refusing offers from the most prestigious galleries."

The telephone rang. My mother. She wants to come up to Paris, on her own. Bad timing, I'm planning to go to Amsterdam for a few days with a friend. It would be a shame to miss each other. She'll put it off till next month. Big kiss and I'll write.

And for now I've still only got the heading.

Since yesterday Delarge can count me amongst his enemies. Linnel is another, in his own way, but that's nothing in comparison to the relentless determination of that girl, the journalist from *Artefact*. She almost stole the show from me yesterday with her public accusations. I've spent a good part of the day trying to get her on the telephone, at her newspaper, and I was clearly not the only one. Towards the end of the afternoon she deigned to reply in the same aggressive mood as the day before.

"Good evening, mademoiselle, I was at the private view yesterday evening and . . ."

"If you're part of the Delarge camp you can hang up straightaway, two lawyers in the same day is enough, I know what constitutes slander . . ."

"No, not at all, I wanted . . ."

"Are you one of the people who's been had? You've

120

bought an Alfonso and you're starting to ask yourself questions? Buy next month's *Artefact*."

"No, that's not it either, I wanted . . ."

"Well, what do you want? Say it! I've got other things to get on with!"

"Can't you shut your mouth for a minute, damn it! I got dragged outside last night too, and I was streaming with blood and so was Delarge, is that good enough for you?"

Slightly stunned silence on the other end. She cleared her throat a couple of times. Her voice softened a little.

"I'm sorry. . . I went with a friend from the paper and I asked him to stay till the end. He told me about the fight . . . was that you?"

"Yes."

"Was it to do with the Cubist?"

"No. Well. . . I don't think so . . ."

"Can we meet?"

Two hours later we're sitting face to face at Le Palatino, a bar not far from my apartment, and the only place in the area where it feels good to lose yourself after midnight. Her name is Béatrice and yesterday she didn't give me time to see her pretty striking face, her dark hair, her curvy figure and especially her smile. To make sure it stays on her face as long as possible I've clamped my bad arm down the side of my body.

"I'm glad you called me, I was sorry I didn't know how to get hold of you when I heard what happened at the end of the evening. I'm interested in anything that can damage Delarge."

"It's a good thing not all art critics are like you."

"That's not really my job, I leave that to the pen-pushers. Have you ever understood anything in art criticism?"

Since yesterday, yes, a bit, and that was thanks to Linnel. But I say no.

"Neither have I. The only thing I'm interested in is the money. Contemporary art doesn't exist without money. I've always wondered how a picture of three blue balls on a beige background can go from nothing to a hundred grand from one year to the next. Well. . . I'm oversimplifying. . . I've made pricing my speciality, and it's fascinating. I love my work."

"I don't understand . . ."

"Have you ever read *Artefact*? I have a whole page every month, I sort of argue a point or I try to talk about all the things that usually get hidden, and it gets me into quite a lot of trouble – fraud, a sudden rise in prices, unreliable estimates, fluctuations influenced by fashion."

"Alfonso?"

I've gone a bit too quickly, and she's sensed it.

"Here I am, talking away . . . and you're not saying anything. It took me a year to put together my story on Alfonso, and I didn't do that just to have it squeezed out of me a fortnight before it's published."

"You're not running any risks with me, I'm not a journalist and I find painting profoundly boring."

"What then? Why Delarge?"

I felt that we were getting into a game of suspicious moves and countermoves, where the winner would have learned the most while giving the least away. And it was going to cost us some time.

"Delarge is hiding things which may have nothing to do with your business with the Cubist. Let's make a deal: I'll tell you my story, and you tell me about your case. We might meet somewhere in the middle. I'll start if you like . . ."

She let me finish, silent, serious and without a trace of a smile. I didn't miss anything out, I don't think. The gentleman with the Stanley knife, the hospital dispatched in a couple of sentences, Delmas, the depot, the Objectivists (whom she'd never heard of), Nico's death, the leaflet and Delarge. I didn't mention billiards and the future I've lost, she wouldn't have understood. I didn't think of the consequences. As a conclusion, I ostentatiously brought my arm down onto the table and she looked searchingly into my eyes.

To allow us a pause, I offered her another glass of Saumur Champigny.

And I suddenly realized I was talking to a girl. A young woman even. As I looked over her curves and her smooth face again, I rediscovered old reflexes. A sort of restraint, policing my every move, but this was completely hypocritical given the fact that, when she got up to buy some cigarettes a moment later, I did everything I could to get a look at her legs. All the contradictions are there – at last I recognize myself. We drank together, in silence, each waiting for the other to make up their mind to talk.

She did.

"I'm going to seem stupid with my Cubist business . . ."

She started to laugh, in a kind way, and I put my arm back down onto my knee – out of some idiotic sense of decency.

"Have you ever heard of Reinhard?" she asks.

"The auctioneer? He was there yesterday."

"I know. Nearly two years ago Delarge announced the

123

sale of virtually the entire output of one Juan Alfonso, a Cubist painter who was completely unknown. With that sort of sale you have to go through an auctioneer who is supposed to authenticate the works, to specify the pricing system and introduce the works to buyers at Drouot by publishing a catalogue. Reinhard handled it so brilliantly, so professionally, that one hundred and fifty pieces were sold in two days."

Coste was pretty well informed.

"Collages, paintings, adorable little sculptures – they were all typical of Cubism, more Cubist than the Cubists, if you see what I mean. The catalogue itself is a masterpiece of ambiguity, no precise dates are given for Alfonso's career; all it does is put forward hypotheses, with plenty of ifs and buts. And that's all it takes to get one over a client base more worried about moving in the right circles than anything else. Everyone's happy, except for Juan Alfonso, who never existed."

"Sorry?"

"Alfonso is a con trick straight out of Edgar Delarge's imagination. It's much cleverer and more lucrative than just coming up with some fakes. He has the work done by a Cubist specialist, and I can tell you that fifty years after their time they're far from glorious. Reinhard whips things up a bit, and the game is won. In my file I've got expert witnesses and an exact reconstruction of the set-up they used to put on the trick. Delarge and Reinhard are a couple of crooks. With what I've got here, they'll go down."

"Aren't you afraid of anything? What if you've been wrong all along?"

"Impossible. You'd never guess how my inquiry began, it was when I was reading the catalogue with a friend: there was a reproduction of two collages, one dated 1911, the other 1923, and they both featured the same design of wallpaper – twelve years apart! There are other blunders like that. The only thing I don't have is the name of the forger."

"Do you think one of his artists could have done this for him?"

"I honestly don't know."

I thought of one individual – a cynical, spiteful one who spends his time sniggering about his benefactor.

"Could it be Linnel?"

"I don't think so. It would be too perfect for my file. When you have an exhibition at the Pompidou Centre you don't get involved with this sort of thing."

I asked her dozens of questions, in a feverish jumble, trying every way I could to connect our two stories – Morand, Alfonso, the Objectivists – and everything became confused in my head.

"Don't get so worked up, the two things may have nothing to do with each other."

"I'll offer you a deal. You give me information, and I'll take care of Delarge."

"What?"

"We could work as a team. You're a journalist, you'll be able to get into places I don't have access to. You look for all the possible connections between Linnel and Morand."

"Oh yes, very funny. What do I get out of this, then? And where should I go, anyway?"

"To the Beaux-Arts. They both went through the place, and at the same time, apparently."

"And what are you going to be up to in the meantime?"

"Me? Nothing. I'll wait like a good boy. But if there's any connection between your story and mine, you'll have everything to gain from it. I'll go and negotiate with Delarge."

"Negotiate what?"

"An interview. The sort of interview you'll never do."

The go-getting young journalist is beginning to express serious doubts about my mental state. Now at last I find her beautiful and perhaps a little vulnerable, and that has put a shred of normality back into the conversation. She is thinking very quickly.

"And how can you prove that you won't forget about me?"

She doesn't wait for an answer but carries on in a quieter voice: "I want to know the forger's name. Look everywhere, get him to cough up some proof, some written proof, something I can publish. After the article's appeared in print there will be a trial, I've been promised it often enough, and that would be one more piece of evidence to show to the court. Irrefutable proof. But that isn't all, I want something else too."

Now I was the one looking at her differently.

"I want an exclusive on your story. Everything. I want to be the first person to talk about it. I can already see my article for September. I'll go to the Beaux-Arts tomorrow. Call me, at home."

I left her, not knowing which of the two of us was the more brutally driven.

*

I didn't have to give my door the ritual kick, it opened with the first turn of the key and it sent a shiver through my hand. I no longer bolt it but I never forget to turn the key a second time. I waited, on the doorstep, for something to happen. From the corridor I felt with my hand to switch on the ceiling light, and I risked a glimpse inside.

Nothing. Not a sound, no sign of a visitor. The mess all over the table looks like my own, the cupboards are closed. My hand is still shaking, and a shudder runs down my spine as I step into my studio. I switch on all the lights, open the window and talk out loud. The adrenaline rush has made me a bit light-headed so I sit on the side of the bed. There's nothing to steal here, apart from a few crumpled pages that prove I've got some idea in the back of my mind. I forget one turn of the key, and all my arrogance flies out of the window, I'm back to the cripple I was that first day, minus the anger. And when I lose that I become the most vulnerable man alive. A surge of anxiety now seems to be coming to an end. This longing for revenge is just a cancer, a gangrene contaminating my most intimate thoughts and feeding off my free will. Nothing better than an illness. Some evenings I curse the fact that I am alone more than everything else.

I slammed the door shut with a good kick but that wasn't enough, I took a shot at the table and chairs, a few things fell to the ground, and I only stopped when my foot was burning with pain. It calmed me down a little. Soon I would find a way of offloading all my negative energy without suffering for it. This evening, tossed between a young woman's evaporated perfume and the impoverished state of my own pride, I'm going to have trouble getting to sleep. I smacked my stump into the edge of the table, I did it without meaning to; perhaps I thought the hand would react. And I lay down, fully clothed, with all the lights on.

At that precise moment I sensed that I was not alone. Barely time to sit back up and look round, and the silhouette loomed up beside the bed with one arm raised – I screamed. A ghost. In the blink of an eye I saw his face again just as it appeared when the statue toppled onto me, his hands wound round my neck, his weight crushed me onto the bed, and the shoelace stopped me crying out, I held out my right arm to scratch at his face but nothing came, with a sharp jerk he pulled the lace towards him and it cut into my flesh, my throat emitted a silent belch, my left arm managed to break free but couldn't reach his eyes, he clamped his hand over my forehead and my eyes hazed over with white, the knot in the shoelace changed angle so that it dug into my windpipe. I felt myself go, suffocated, all at once.

Passed out, in that vice.

Eyes bulging open . . .

And, right next to me, through the fog, I saw the billiard cue within reach.

I gave a thrust of my hips to heave myself towards it, he saw it and tried to hold my arm down, the shoelace barely slackened, he lost his balance and toppled to the floor with me. I coughed so hard it almost ripped my throat out, he had time to get up and tighten the lace again, almost blind now, I grabbed the cue, and the handle knocked into his forehead, without any power behind it, he hardly even looked up, the lace squeezed me tight again, and I spun the cue in the air to bringing it crashing onto his face with the full force of my anger. I coughed until I nearly spat my guts out, I found the strength to strike again, four, maybe five times, but I soon ran out of breath, my legs couldn't hold me any longer, and I sat down.

My breath came back in halting gasps, I held my hand over my burning windpipe and forced myself to breathe through my nose. I had to wait – suffocating, motionless and with my neck twisting in pain – while my lungs filled. I saw him crawling, dazed, towards the door, moving incredibly slowly. I belched out the most impossible sound, I would have liked to tell him, but I could only moan like a mute, so I thought, very hard, in the hope that he would hear me. This has got to stop, you and me. . . What are you doing? Come back. . . We have to finish this this evening. . . Where are you going . . .?

He only took his hands away from his face so that he could cling to the table legs, they slipped, slick with blood, and there was nothing I could do when he stood up. A neighbour called from outside. With my hoarse cough and my tears, and with the shoelace hanging from my neck, I couldn't work out how to drag myself away from the bed.

He lurched into the furniture. I didn't watch him leave. I just looked at the floor and followed the sinuous progress of his trails of blood.

And I started to cry, and to suffocate even more, and to cry again.

I don't know how long it went on but, centuries later, I saw my neighbour from across the landing peeping, ashen-faced, through the half-open door. He said something about noise, blood and the police. I wanted to reply but the pain in my throat flared again and it reminded me of hospital, of the staples in my mouth and of being deprived of speech. I slowly shook my head, I pointed my finger at the door then leaned my cheek gently against the back of my hand to tell him to go to bed.

In the aura of violence that still reverberated around the room, he sensed that he should categorically not disturb my newfound calm. My serene lunacy frightened him. He closed the door without a sound.

5

I almost left without cleaning up the blood. On my knees, I ran the floor cloth over the splashes, they were still fresh. I was simply anticipating my homecoming and the dismal surprise of seeing my studio splattered with scabs. I picked up my bag, stuffed a few clothes into it and set off outside in the mild dawn air, without really knowing where my longing for nothingness would take me. A desire for revenge, a desire for peace, should I go up the street or down the street – I'm at a loss.

He should have stayed. What a prick I've been not to have thought of a prosthesis. I have regrets after each of our encounters. A good hook, a really old-fashioned, really pointy one. Because actually, now that I come to think of it, that sort of attachment would be much more use to me now than a hand.

If I head towards République, I will have a better chance of finding a room. Two or three days, maybe more, definitely not less.

The gentleman wanted me dead. He's got it in for my memory, which is full of brand new images, for that last copy of *Attempt 30*, for my tendency to go round talking about it and for my nose with its powers of resistance. He must think of me, sometimes. I would pay a high price to know how he sees me.

My throat brings me back down to earth every time I swallow. But my voice is coming back. I let my vocal cords run through from deep notes to high ones.

130

I feel had, overcooked all over. Maybe that's the third-degree-burns feeling Briançon mentioned.

Hotel du Carreau du Temple. The first one with its sign still lit up. At six o'clock in the morning, I will be waking the night porter. No, not actually, I can see him in the foyer surrounded by baskets of croissants.

He comes over. A room? There's only one left, with a double bed; I take it and pay for two days in advance. What time for the wake-up call? No wake-up call, no. We don't serve breakfast after 10.30. Never mind, thank you.

Room 62. I had a hot shower in the dark, to avoid seeing myself in the mirror with the red wheals around my neck. The nape of my neck is still hurting. I got lost in that big double bed. It would have been impossible to find me there.

*

The white and red come to a gentle kiss in a corner of the baize . . . I'm afraid I will never be able to rest again without being haunted by them. I always have the same dream, play the same point. Nothing symbolic, nothing mysterious, no key to anything. It is all pathetically prosaic, and the moment of waking all the more painful for it.

Before getting dressed again, I dare to look at myself in the wardrobe mirror. From behind, from the front. It's the first time I have seen myself completely naked since the amputation. My face is a bit puffy, but I can't tell now whether that's from yesterday or the day before. I have put on a bit of weight. I don't know if it's an optical illusion, but I think my right arm has shrunk slightly in comparison to my left. Atrophying, probably. It will be a chicken wing soon if I don't do

131

anything about it. My neck is neither purple nor black, but just red, with flakes of dusty skin that stick to my fingers when I touch it. The pinkish ring left by the shoelace is very clear. There are yellowing bruises on my shoulders and thighs. The whole thing looks like a badly digested Mondrian ... Briançon wouldn't be able to do anything to sort it out. Only a restorer could help. Jean-Yves. He would come along with his little case and his gloves and peer at me with his linen tester to isolate the damaged fibre. Then over in a corner, lying on the ground, he would spend hours finding the exact nuance of pigments, and – with the patience of a saint – he would touch up the injured areas with the tip of his paintbrush. I really liked Jean-Yves with his little round glasses and his moustache. However much I talked to him about his work, he always managed to shift the conversation to tennis. In the end he specialized in whites, people would call him from all over Europe to reunify the background of a painting. I would never have guessed that between white and white there was such an incredible variety of whites.

*

At about four in the afternoon, when I ran out of patience, I rang Béatrice and suggested we meet at the Palatino, in case she had something for me. She suggested it would be better if I dropped by her apartment, and I eventually accepted. Before hanging up she did ask me why I had hesitated. "No reason," I replied.

She lives in another world, on the Rive Gauche, in the Rue de Rennes, somewhere I never venture.

"What's happened to you?"

She brought her hand up to my neck, and I turned up my collar.

"Probably tell you some time. Did you go?"

"How about coming in before asking questions . . . ?"

I was expecting a light, expensive-looking place with wall-to-wall carpeting, Ikea furniture and Venetian blinds. And I find myself between two different computer monitors, piles of daily papers, and walls lined with books and frescoes of press cuttings, collages of photos, magazine covers taped straight onto the wall, the poster for a Cremonini Exhibition with an image of naked, faceless children. A table dotted with ashtrays spewing cigarette ends, a pizza in its cardboard packaging. Not untidiness or slovenliness: no, more an impression of speed, an insatiable, bulimic appetite for information, a need to say that the world is here, everywhere.

"You don't miss anything," I said.

"Sit down wherever you can, look . . . here . . ."

The edge of the sofa, near the telephone and the answering machine. She comes back with two cups and a teapot, without asking if I would like it, and sits down at my feet. When she bends over to fill the cups I get a glimpse of her breasts. She hands me a saucer with one eye still on the corner of a newspaper stranded on the floor. When you find a girl as frenetic as this, as avid as this, you have to marry her very, very quickly, I thought.

"The Beaux-Arts, child's play! The lowliest freelancer could have done it. I claimed I was doing a paper on the glorious artists they had produced, starting with Linnel, because of the connection with the Pompidou Centre . . . I had a stroke of luck, there was an old secretary who was tickled pink to be interviewed, thirty years' worth of paperwork, she was like a computer crossed with an old mother hen."

"What did she tell you about Linnel?"

"Aaaaaah Linnel, dear little Alain, such talent! And a practical joker too, if you only knew what he put us through! Every year he developed more and more sophisticated ways of ragging the new intake, and his imagination very nearly got us into trouble with the police! Apparently he made the new students –"

"Is this really important?" I interrupted.

"No, but it's funny. Well, anyway, he did his six years there, the tutors passed everything they knew on to him, despite the mucking about. The absolute prototype of the student who does nothing and knows how to do everything. It's maddening and it's seductive, and it demoralizes the other people in the same intake. Except for Morand, his inseparable friend, who was more reticent, harder working. 'Nice but not very talkative,' the old woman told me. 'He was interested in little things, crazes, calligraphy, miniatures, but the academic drawing lessons didn't really inspire him.' He was the most discreet of the gang of four."

She has left a pause, deliberately, to make me rise to the bait. Four . . . Four . . . The James brothers, the Daltons. It's the right number for a gang. I've got two of them already. I'm afraid of having three. I know one with a talent for appearing just when he's not expected. Given his age and his obsessions, he could be the third. The gentleman. My appointed duelling partner.

"Claude Reinhard," she says.

"What?"

"Yes, the auctioneer. He's very different. He only stayed there three years, the son of Adrien Reinhard, from the renowned Reinhard business, the most –"

"I know, I know, and so . . ."

"He tried himself out at the Beaux-Arts out of defiance, as a way of flouting his father's authority. Daddy handles paintings that cost thousands, he wants me to carry on with his precious business, well no, I'll *make* paintings that cost thousands, and he'll be forced to give his expert opinion on them one day. So he pitched up at the Quai Malaquais in a convertible, and very soon fell in with the two old hands. They all left at the same time, at the end of '63. For the final year they were inseparable, the gang of four really gelled that year."

I still have a chance, a joker to play for the fourth member.

"Would you like to have supper here?"

"And the fourth?"

"I've made courgettes in cheese sauce."

She can tell I couldn't give a stuff. And I'm wondering whether I really don't give a stuff, I'm wondering whether the fourth man is actually who I think he is, whether she made this courgette dish for me, whether I'm not about to speed up our engagement, whether I'm going back to Biarritz, or whether she chose courgettes because you can eat them with one hand, without a knife.

"I'm intrigued by this story of yours," I say, "go on . . . please."

"No, from now on it's your story that intrigues me. It's going to be my article for September. The fourth member was called Bettrancourt, Julien Bettrancourt. And – in spite of Reinhard and his money, in spite of Linnel and his brilliantly perverse ideas – he was very much the leader of the gang. The old girl tried to evade the question, bad memories for her and for the whole establishment. 'There's no need for you to mention him in your newspaper, young lady . . .' she could have been describing Bluebeard, the way she talked."

I've moved a little closer to her face to try and catch the smell of her. She's realized this and hasn't back away.

135

"Fatherless. Obscure. A puny man who instilled terror in the Beaux-Arts and other places too. He never knew when to stop, took things to extremes, and the management always suspected that he had vandalized the premises, some frescoes, with cryptic slogans that completely terrorized everyone. He was apparently a gifted orator and he paralysed the poor pupils with their pitiful folders of watercolours under their arms."

I thought of the pamphlet again.

" 'He had a bad influence on the other three, it was a shame to see . . .' Oh, really . . . the three of them were in love with him, more like. They chose him as their mentor, their guru. He must have been very charismatic, don't you think?"

"Would you have given him courgettes in cheese sauce?"

"No, grilled steak."

Actually, now I'm no longer sure I will marry her. She is running her hand through her hair without taking her green eyes off me. Light green.

"Linnel had a good chance of winning the Prix de Rome, but when Bettrancourt dumped the place, the other three followed. Linnel, the teachers' pet; Morand, the lunatic; Reinhard the daddy's boy; and Bettrancourt, the terrorist, a blank year in their biographies, from '63 to '65. Frank, ambitious, insolent. There are your Objectivists."

Yes. No doubt about it. College friends, 1963, every dream imaginable, a convertible, white shirts, afternoons at the Palette café, evenings at the Select, endless discussions about American painters. One day they decide to take the first step, to break away from the comforts of home and burn their false hopes. If they had been older or more patient they would have called it the 'old world'. They came and went too soon. The

Objectivists lasted only one summer. Morand flew off over the Atlantic, Reinhard stepped into line, and the young Alain Linnel became just Linnel.

"At the ripe old age of thirty, do you think we really understand it all?"

"Yes and no," I say. "In those days I was climbing onto chairs to watch the people in the café opposite playing billiards. My only memory of 1968 is the Mexico Olympics."

"I won a chattering prize at nursery school in 1964. I'll swear on my press card that that's true."

"How old are you?"

"Twenty-seven," she says.

"Congratulations ... If you carry on at this rate, throwing yourself into your work, in three years' time you'll be working on a big daily paper, in five you will have taken the arts editor's job, then you'll be editor-in-chief and in ten years you'll have the Pulitzer Prize."

"That's right, and in twenty years I'll be doing the obituaries in a crappy local paper. Stop making fun of me."

How long is it since I've seen a girl this close up? It must run into years, I think. At least a year. A woman who came to look round the gallery. She never got to see me in the evenings. I would go to her house after midnight, or at the weekend, before going off to play. She got fed up in the end.

"I like your vocation as a whistle-blower."

"Well, life gets boring otherwise, doesn't it?"

I almost kissed her when she got up to put the tray away. Shame. I wanted to know if it would have any effect on me and whether, somewhere inside, something would have quivered a bit.

"Is there no way of knowing what happened to the

ringleader?" I asked. I still haven't given up hope of recognizing that bastard gentleman in him.

"No, the old woman didn't know, and she certainly didn't mind. When I really pushed her, she found his old address in the archives – I could give it to you. And I got Linnel's through the paper. As for Delarge, not a chance, you can only get hold of him at the gallery. You'll have to make do with that. That's what I've managed to find today."

"And you had time to make a cheese sauce?" I said.

"Do you want some or not?"

I don't answer. She kneels close to me and pulls at my right sleeve to draw the arm nearer to her. She is staring into my eyes as if trying to hypnotize a cobra, and I have no idea what she wants to do with my bad arm. All of a sudden I feel frightened.

"Could we have supper . . . ?" I say.

She pushes the tips of her fingers inside the sleeve. She strokes the rounded, bony end.

"It's smooth . . ."

I didn't understand, I wanted to pull my arm back, but she stopped me, gripping the stump with both her hands.

"You . . . you really like what you can't have," I said.

In reply she simply dropped her lips against mine for a second. Then the weight of her whole body onto my stomach.

This is going too quickly.

I'm not prepared for it.

What's this going to look like when we're naked, a Rubens on a Mondrian? My primary colours and her classical curves. Why is she doing this? I can neither reject her nor take hold of her hips properly.

Everything is jumbled together, her strange, crawling action against my chest, the twinkle of an eye and the

138

matt surface of skin, my Surrealist amputation sliding against her armpit, and my third eye up above, watching the tableau. That is solid proof that I don't want this. I would never have guessed that the dysfunction could be so far-reaching. She took her dress off in the few seconds when my eyes were closed, when I saw all sorts of other things, violent contrasts of darkness and purity, paradoxes of reality and illogical nonsense. Her nudity drew me out of that shapeless nightmare, she offered me the raw material of her flesh, ready to be re-sculpted from head to foot. When she took my hand and laid it on the sketched curve at the small of her back, I understood that the work was already done, that someone else was the author of this magnificent tactile landscape. But I didn't resist the urge to take everything back to the beginning. A blind man and a trunk in clay. I now lay on top of her, so as not to miss anything, not the rough or the smooth, the curves or the angles. I quickly realized that my one hand was enough. Better than that, now that it was alone, it seemed to caress more tenderly, with more precision.

"Wait . . . I like bed better," she said.

I followed her. We lay down. And that was when everything that had been missing came back. The smell of bodies, the breathing, the sighs, that hungering for someone else and the countless reflexes of desire. Of love. My third eye disappeared, along with every kind of abstraction. Now I was thinking only of her.

*

"Tomorrow?" she asked.

". . . What about tomorrow?"

"Delarge."

"I don't know. Surely . . ."

We waitcd until the sun was really up before leaving her apartment. Out in the street, she whispered one last thing in my ear.

"Written proof . . ."

While I waited for her to disappear round the corner I tightly clenched my phantom fist.

6

What a waste of time. Huddled behind the staircase of entrance B at 59 Rue Barbette, all I saw was the secretary's red hair leaving the office to disappear into the backroom. Delarge eventually emerged from his three brick columns at about ten pm, and they gathered up all their bits and pieces, together, before leaving. He switched on the electronic system that works the alarm and brings down the metal shutter. She locked up the gallery, and they walked right past me. I went back to the hotel, cursing the carrot-topped doorkeeper and her shed-load of overtime. I even set about trying to find a radical way of confining her to bed over the next few days.

It seemed absurd to spend another night just up the road from home, but I still couldn't make up my mind to go back to my studio. Delmas is going to have trouble getting hold of me, should he need to.

The next day, instead of waiting till the evening like a good boy for a second attempt, I ventured into the southern suburbs, in Chevilly-Larue, to have a prowl around Bettrancourt's former address. I found a Hélène Bettrancourt in the phonebook, but I didn't think it was a good idea to announce my arrival or to make an anonymous phone call. It's a small house squeezed between a hypermarket and a car wrecking yard with a black forecourt stinking of diesel. I wondered whether a gentleman could live there. I had to conclude that he couldn't; given that, I went ahead and rang the bell without pacing and fretting around the house.

A wrinkled face behind the curtain, an engine whining hoarsely in the scrap yard, an Alsatian called back by the old woman. The dog obeys her promptly.

"I'm trying to find news of Julien!"

I quickly grasped that it would have been incredibly easy – and incredibly shameful – to sweet-talk the old woman. Old mother Bettrancourt. But how else would I get in?

She doesn't seem surprised or frightened. She said I should follow her inside, because it would be easier, because there was too much noise from the cars, because she was bored, and because it's always a pleasure seeing a friend of Julien's. I was a friend, wasn't I? Oh yes, Madame, very much so, since our days at the Beaux-Arts, that was right back in . . ."

"'63," she says tartly.

The dog is sniffing my legs, the dining room can't have changed in fifty years, and there can't be anyone much but her around the place. She tells me to sit at the table and takes out a bottle of liqueur and two glasses, and it all feels like the most well rehearsed ritual. I start thinking about her implacable young son. Nothing I can see here really fits with the character Béatrice described. Another engine roars, and this time it sounds as if the mechanic thinks he's on the start line for Le Mans.

"I hate cars, but I can't leave the house. All that I have left of Julien is here. So . . . Are you a real painter too?"

What should I tell her? No, of course, I'm in imports and exports. I'm sure that when I leave the place she still won't have seen I have an arm missing.

"You've been here before, haven't you? I think I

recognize you. He had so many friends at college. And they would tramp through here and talk and talk, if his father could have seen it . . ."

"I remember a few friends, Alain Linnel, Etienne Morand, and some others . . ."

"Do you remember Alain? We could give him a ring if you like, oh yes, he'd be so happy to see an old friend from those days . . ."

I have to get up when she picks up the telephone.

"No, no, I can't stay long."

"Well, come back tomorrow evening, then. Yes, it will actually be Friday. At about six o'clock, he never gets here before that . . ."

"It's nice of him to come and see you. Does he come often?"

"Oh, too much even. He must have other things to do . . . he worries. He really wanted me to have Bobby to keep me company . . . He bought him for me. He wants to find me a house in the country, but I can't leave all this. He's so kind. It's so difficult, painting, I mean . . . how many years does it take before it becomes a real job? And there's Alain – I'm sure he's a real painter and that he'll sell his paintings one day. I'm sure of it."

"Well, Julien did beautiful work at college too."

She gave a little grunt, almost of amusement.

"Do you really think so?"

"Yes."

"Perhaps . . . Mind you, I never said anything to stop him, he did what he liked. I respected everything, you know. Even if I didn't understand it, I knew he really loved it, that he was sincere . . . He seemed so focused on what he was doing. As if it was something serious. But why were the things he did so . . . so gloomy . . .? He wasn't a gloomy boy, you know . . . So why did he do those . . . those things? You see, I think artists should make sculptures that make you forget all the misery . . . it's a sort of optimism . . . Paintings that do you good . . . I don't know how to put it . . . But I've kept everything. It's all I've got left since the accident. Would you like to see them?"

"Yes."

"It's my own museum. Apart from Alain, there aren't many visitors . . ."

She said that to make me smile. I follow her into a ground-floor bedroom with a window overlooking the scrap yard.

"It was his studio, he used to say."

A completely different smell, a hint of grease and lubricating oil which has persisted over the years, and it's hardly surprising when you have a look at what's in there. At least a hundredweight of old iron, mobiles hanging from the ceiling, little architectural creations of woven, soldered metal stuck onto wooden plaques. Those are what you notice straightaway. All the same format, rectangles of wood, eleven inches by twenty-four. The first thing that strikes you is a feeling of precision, the arrangement of those metallic pieces must surely obey some well defined system. Anything but random.

"He called these his portraits. What on earth did they teach them at the Beaux-Arts . . .?"

Portraits.

I can't resist my curiosity, the urge to hold one up in front of the wall. Then another, then all of them. That's how you should look at them, if you go by the pencilled arrows on the back of the wood. And that's not all. Each of them is accompanied by a name, still in pencil. My heart has started thumping, but this is neither fear nor distress.

144

"Alain 62". "Etienne 62". "Claude 62". And others that I don't know.

"Alain 62". The features are taking shape, gradually, in this tiny jungle of metal. The left eye is a little spiral, part of a clock. A cocoa tin which has been cut open and hammered out suggests the forehead, and a meticulous and complicated tangle of bicycle chain, a rusty smile. In places there are touches of engine grease which make the features gleam. A feeling of fullness, a rounded cheek in cast iron, a nose immaculately carved out of a knife blade eaten away by rust.

The more I look at him, the more . . .

"Be careful . . . Especially with the things that are on the table."

The things have been put there carefully, posed. And it's obvious why you have to be careful – they are hostile. An aluminium mould encrusted with razor blades. It would be impossible to pick it up without drawing blood. A telephone handset bristling with rusting spikes. A basket with a sharpened billhook as a handle.

"The number of times he injured himself . . ."

Through the window I can see the broken fence that once separated the garden from the scrap yard and, in the middle of it, the carcasses of two cars hanging vertically, one slotted against the other.

Embracing.

"The boss next door let him play with the wrecks. I was a bit ashamed with the neighbours but it made him so happy . . . Then last year the boss wanted to have a tidy up, and Alain bought this from him. What you can see down there. I hate cars."

She wants to get me back to the sitting room, which is a shame. I could have done with another hour getting to know all this, finding other faces, and risking my remaining hand on those impossible objects.

"And have you seen Morand since the accident?"

"Little Etienne . . . No, I think he went to America, and the other one never came back either, I've forgotten his name, the one with the beautiful red car. I hate cars. They were always holed up here, those three, talking, arguing even, sometimes."

She leaves a little pause. I bite my lip.

"And that evening they went off in the little Renault. He didn't have much luck, my Julien. The others came away unharmed. Come back on a Friday evening. Alain will be here, he would really like that."

The gallery looks shut, and I haven't seen any signs of movement inside. The only thing that gives me hope is the fact that the metal shutter isn't down, and this time I've changed my lookout post. Halfway up to the first floor on staircase B there's a dressmaking workshop typical of this part of Paris, and so far I haven't had to suffer any comings and goings . . . while I wait for someone to deign to turn up.

Delarge, alone, keys in hand, appeared at about eleven pm. I have flown down the stairs intent on pouncing on him before he has a chance to react. I run as fast as I can across the empty little courtyard, he is bent forward, turning the key to the security system. His back is offered up to me, the shutter is a third of the way down, and I put my arm over his shoulder as if to surprise an old friend. Gently. The triangular tip of the Stanley knife just reaches his carotid artery.

"Would you open it, please?" I ask calmly.

He shrieks in surprise. Flabbergasted, he recognizes

me, he stammers, everything happens very quickly, he stands back up and turns the key the other way.

"Can you lower the shutter from the inside?" I ask, pressing the blade a little deeper against his throat.

He puts up no resistance and gives a hysterical little "yes". His face is distorted with fear, and he shakes as he handles the lock. My heart is hardly beating any faster, both my arms feel full of strength, the metal stays clamped under his chin without deviating a hair's breadth. The fact that I have waited twenty-four hours has only intensified my loathing. Yesterday I hadn't yet met that little woman living on the rusted altar of memories. I won't take it any more, this assassination of gentleness and kindness. Yesterday I might have been hesitant and haphazard.

He put the lights on in the gallery before I even expressed the wish.

"Don't . . . don't hurt me!"

I can feel him there, at the tip of my blade, paralysed with terror, and that makes my job easier. So long as he's whimpering like a little kid, I can play it easy. Stuck between the blade and my chest, he walks, steady and straight, till he gets to the reception desk. Now at last I can enjoy total impunity, protected by the metal shutter.

"Lie down on your front, on the floor!"

He obeys. I put the slipknot at the end of the shoe-lace over the table leg, lifting the table with my shoulder. It takes a couple of attempts, and with my teeth I open up the second knot, at the other end of the lace.

"Lift your head up . . . Come over to the table leg, fuck it!"

I slip his head gently into the loop and pull it sharply. He doesn't cry out. There is no more than four inches of string between the table leg and his neck. I watch him, cowering on the ground, held back by the painfully short lead, like a terrorized dog waiting to be kicked.

"You see, I use the same weapons as your killer, a Stanley knife and string, and all with one hand."

"Don't hurt me."

"I have you to thank for this stump, don't I?"

"What do you want?"

"An interview."

He opens his eyes wide, he looks like a madman . . . or like someone looking at a madman.

"The man who cut off my hand and who came to my studio to finish the job, he's one of yours, isn't he? Answer me, quickly."

He screamed out a sound that could have meant either yes or no.

"That's not clear enough."

He swallows several times and tries to get to his knees, but the shoelace won't allow him to.

"I won't say anything."

He tucks his head between his shoulders and closes his eyes tight. Like a temperamental child. A foul-mouthed brat. Stubborn.

"I . . . I won't tell you anything . . ."

I registered a hint of surprise. I didn't know what to do. He repeats his words slowly, he won't tell me, he won't tell me.

That's just my luck. Everything was going so well, and I've ended up with this ball of fear under the table. He is even more afraid of letting slip some sort of admission than of violence. And I am perfectly incapable of committing that violence. I have absolutely no faith in myself in that department. With the gentleman there's no problem, in fact – quite the opposite – I would have liked to do a lot more. But with a man thirty years older than me, on his knees, I'm lost. Actually, at that private view, it was Linnel I should have punched. I was drunk.

Time and hesitation are playing against me, I'm beginning to feel I'm losing him, that he isn't afraid of me.

I mustn't get this wrong.

In a couple of seconds he will almost be smiling.

I have sat down on the floor next to him. I have forced myself to think that this man has ruined the rest of my life, and that only yesterday he wanted to see me dead.

I notice the paintings on the wall and go over so that I can see them better.

"Is art really a passion?" I ask out loud.

No reply.

"This is your private collection, isn't it?"

Not a word.

"A real passion or a good investment?"

Silence.

I take out a lighter, bought for the occasion. An idea I nabbed from the gentleman, like the rest of my arsenal.

I'm not going to draw blood from this piece of shit. It's a question of mental health. But I know as well as the next man that there's an almost infinite range of tortures. He knows it too, and there's a new gleam of anxiety in his eye. I grasp the lighter and bring the flame up to the Linnel.

"It won't . . . it won't do you any good!" he says in his cracked voice.

"A passion? Or just a source of money?"

"Stop . . . I won't say anything!"

The flame eats into the middle of the canvas, a round circle forms and a tongue of flame starts to appear.

"Stop! You're . . . you're mad! Don't do that! We didn't . . . have anything against you . . . particularly . . . We just wanted *Attempt 30*."

The canvas is burning up, nice and slowly.

"You got in the way, he . . . he reacted . . . No one knew that you . . . that you would try to find out more . . . your questions . . . You knew the Objectivists existed . . . And we're all trying to forget them . . ."

He begs me, once again, to take the flame away. What was the point? The shrivelled thing was unsaleable now. Or was it just the sentimental value. He had chosen a painting he liked from the studio of his friend and protégé.

"Go on . . . tell me what happened after the exhibition in '64."

"I wanted to look after them . . . to get them to work . . . oh and . . . Do what you like, I won't say any more."

The Linnel has been reduced to a black cavity. I mustn't give up now, Delarge is about to crack, he is under my power again. Who should it be next? I have quite a choice.

"Which should I burn first? The Kandinsky or the Braque?"

Delarge puts his head in his hands, he begs me, and heaves like a donkey leaning against its halter, dragging the table.

"Don't move, Delarge," I say, waving the lighter.

He freezes, horror in his eyes.

"They had a ringleader . . . a failure who needed the group to hide his own mediocrity. I wasn't interested in him but the creep had the others under his thumb. I wanted Linnel and Morand, they were the ones I was really interested in. I'd been to their studios, Linnel had everything it takes to be a great artist, and Morand had a dexterity and a precision which could have been

150

useful to me some day. No connection with what their ringleader was doing! Pathetic art! But, there you are, they didn't do anything without him, without his blessing, like the word of God! They were young, stupid and easily influenced. Don't do that, please, keep that flame away! I'll give you everything you want . . ."

With all his whinging he has just answered my question. Passion or money, the two are perfectly compatible. I have flicked the lighter off.

"What did you do with Bettrancourt?"

The way he looks me up and down says it all. With a question like that I was confident he would get an idea of the ground I had already covered in the utterly forgettable History of Contemporary Art.

"He was the one who founded the group, he was always the one who refused my offers . . . but I got them in the end. It didn't take the other three long to understand, groups never last very long, I told them they wouldn't get far by refusing to sell, that their little adolescent rebellion would peter out, and then, money . . . Linnel was the first to bite, Reinhard didn't need it but he followed suit, and Morand held out a bit longer."

He tries to loosen the shoelace before going on.

"Bettrancourt would never have given in, he was becoming a hindrance. He would have preferred to die, for ethical reasons, yes, ethical . . . Mad. I convinced each of the others to put a painting before the acquisitions board without his knowing, to prove to them that their paintings were worth a lot. And that was just a beginning. When the state paid out, they finally understood. The word of God started to lose its edge, Bettrancourt was losing his grip, and their individual ambitions gradually emerged. And do you really want to know? I'm proud I did that. Thanks to me, they painted instead of sinking into oblivion."

151

This whirl of information from him makes me giddy. I feel as if the fog has finally cleared above the gorge and I can look down into it at last. There are so many things I would like to ask him that not one of them comes to me spontaneously, and we sit there in silence for a moment.

"Now I'm going to tell you what happened next. Whatever you may say, you know exactly what happened to Bettrancourt. You urged the other three to break away from him, one way or another. The group was destined to a great career and, I mean, why not work as a threesome instead of a foursome, given that they'd already found an idea and a system? You made them shine far brighter than young students could dream of. And all so quickly. And if people are so keen to forget the Objectivists now it's because the way they ended was radical. Bettrancourt frightened you, he could have done anything. They eliminated the leader, a car crash, so simple. October '64. Am I right?"

He looks up and smirks in amazement.

"You knew . . . Did you force me to tell you what you already knew?"

"I'd sort of guessed. What I don't understand is why they didn't carry on with the group."

"Oh well, neither do I. After the accident they didn't even know themselves whether or not they were guilty. Morand really coped badly afterwards, the guilt, something stupid like that . . . One morning he announced to the other two that he was leaving for the States, that the Objectivists could carry on without him. Reinhard was frightened, he abandoned his paintbrushes to go back to his father's business."

"And Linnel carried on on his own, under your protection. That explains your difficult relationship. A collaboration built on a dead body, what a great foundation . . . But twenty years later Morand comes back – dead but very much there. An exhibition is devoted to him and, unintentionally, one Objectivist painting is included, a reminder. It brings back all sorts of forgotten stuff, and it's terrible timing, just as Linnel is about to be exhibited at the Pompidou Centre, with a public commission into the bargain."

"No one knew what had happened to him, and then Coste brought him back to life. That painting shouldn't have been exhibited, it harboured various kinds of proof, we panicked. After that we had to carry on with the job, the painting that had been sold to the nation. And it was all over, not a trace left of that wretched group. And then . . ."

"And then there was me."

I give a weary sigh. I'm exhausted. And I've had enough. I feel like leaving and abandoning him there, hanging on the end of his leash. I can't see what else to do. I just want to be left alone.

Alone.

My desire for revenge amounts to that.

"What are you going to do with me . . .?"

"Me? Nothing."

As I say that, I think of the journalist again, and her written proof. By threatening to reduce the Braque to shreds I got the forger's name. I'm sorry that it wasn't Linnel. A name that didn't mean anything to me. But, mind you, if he'd had another name . . .

I smirked.

"Tell me, Monsieur Delarge, your forger, he has other talents, doesn't he?"

"What . . . what do you mean by that?"

"He does quite a lot of favours for you. And he wears a tweed suit and a Burberry, doesn't he?"

"It's true . . . but you could burn my whole collection

and I couldn't tell you more than that. He's got nothing to do with the Beaux-Arts. I hardly know anything about his past. I think he used to paint. He's already had problems with the police, but that's none of my business. He won't be exhibited anywhere any more. I find ways to get work for him."

An artist in his own way, I thought. I rifled through the next office, and all I found was a letter from Reinhard referring to an order for a hundred and fifty pieces. I think that will do. Béatrice will have to manage. It's nothing to do with me any more.

"I'm going to make you an offer: it all stops here. I know too much about you, Reinhard and Linnel, I'm a living danger, I know that . . . I don't want to go on waiting for another visit from the gentleman – who won't miss me next time. You should know that if anything happens to me, the journalist from *Artefact* will publish a complete article on what's happened to me. She's got it in her power, hasn't she?"

"That . . . that bitch . . ."

I didn't like that. Really not. One word too many, again.

In a flash I take the Kandinsky watercolour down and lie it on the floor. Delarge is gasping, watching in fascination, more childlike than ever. I light up the lighter again, he howls for mercy and I like it.

"You can't do that! You don't know, you couldn't!"

And I suddenly realize that he's right. That there is no point stupidly burning a work of art of that calibre. I'm not really sure what a Kandinsky represents. I don't know anything about it. I'm a crass philistine. I just know it's a name that can silence a room when it is mentioned, that he was there at the very beginnings of abstract art and that he discovered it when he was transfixed in admiration of one of his own paintings

154

that had been hung upside down. So for me to burn something like that, well, it seemed a bit mean. A gesture like that would have been fundamentally lacking in any feeling of pleasure.

So I change my mind, or rather, my form of torture. Next to the visitors' book there are some pens, felt tips and a thick marker. And I thought to myself: Go on, Antoine, this will only happen once in your life.

I took the lid off the marker with my teeth and brandished it in the air, in the top left-hand corner of the canvas. Behind me I heard a heartrending cry, which only served to encourage me.

"Be quiet! I'm not going to deface your painting, I'm just going to add a few bits and bobs."

Blue background, green circles with lines through them, overlapping geometric figures, triangles in lozenges and crosses in ovals in every possible colour.

I've put three black daisies bobbing out of a trapezium. Next to a crescent-moon shape I've populated a whole area with five-pointed stars. My left hand is wonderful. It's touching up a Kandinsky. I just had to have faith in it. With one of the circles I couldn't help regressing to childhood, and I've drawn a mouth and two eyes, with irises and pupils.

I drop the marker on the floor and turn round.

"There we are, isn't it better like that?"

7

Leave Paris.

Sooner or later I'm going to have to go to Biarritz. My parents deserve better than a letter. Anyway, they would have come. A whole century of painting wasn't any help sketching out the note to them. Nothing but rather arcane drafts. But now that I can distinguish between being one-armed and being left-handed, I will be able to explain to them and perhaps even play the whole thing down.

Another couple of things to sort out, ring Béatrice, finalize a cast-iron account of the last few days I've spent in Paris, with the Polaroid of *Attempt 8* as a bonus. It can act as an illustration. Should I really bother going back to my studio? Or even letting Delmas know? No. He would know how to find me if I became indispensable. All I want is for him to go on marking time for a while, for him to leave everyone in peace, I don't feel like talking, testifying and justifying my every action. It would be bound to cause me a fair amount of grief, what with hiding evidence and physical assaults, not to mention my obstinate attempts to dispense justice myself.

Justice . . . I will never get back what I've lost, and the worst of it is I will end up getting used to it. And forgetting billiards. All too soon. This great surge of furious activity has worn me out.

I slept for more than twenty-four hours. On my body's orders. A physiological need to be alone. The man on night duty made me a sandwich, I had a beer with him and I came back up to my room in the early hours. I waited one more night, trying to think back through the whole of this saga, and I sorted everything out. Peace. I have restored myself all on my own, I'm gradually going back to my original colours. For the first time in a long while I've succeeded in making the time I wake up coincide with morning. My biological clock has righted itself all on its own, and it's telling me that it's high time I got out of here.

Béatrice must be getting impatient, I should have rung her as I left Delarge but I so badly wanted to be on my own, waiting for the fever to drop.

It's only ten o'clock in the morning. There's someone different on duty today, I don't know him. Four hundred francs for three nights; as he gives me my change he doesn't take his eyes off my right sleeve and doesn't deign to look me in the eye, not even once.

"Can I make a phone call within Paris?"

He puts the telephone down in front of me and comes out from behind his desk. And, just when I was beginning to lose my aggressive tendencies, I wonder whether I will ever fit in with other people again.

First I rang the paper, but when I got the answering machine I realized it was Sunday. And when you're not expecting it, it comes as a shock. Sunday . . .

I try her at home.

"Béatrice? It's Antoine."

". . . Yes, just a second . . ."

It takes much longer than that. I was expecting a gasp of surprise or irritation, even a bollocking because it had taken me so long.

"Are you okay?" she asks.

"I don't know. I'm going away, to the country . . . and I wanted to tell you . . ."

"Where are you?"

"Um . . . at the hotel, but I won't be here long . . ."

"Shall we meet?"

Strange. I'm no longer sure exactly who I've got on the other end of the line. I would have thought she would make me spill a good part of the beans over the phone.

"What's going on? Am I disturbing something?"

"No, no. Come over to my apartment."

"Haven't got time, I want to get out of here. Let's meet at the Gare de Lyon in half an hour. At the buffet restaurant."

She waits a moment before agreeing. And before hanging up, just like that . . .

I have a horrible feeling she wasn't alone. The fever soars again in a flash. I must have missed something while I was asleep. Some detail which has reawakened my paranoia just when I was coming back up to the surface.

I leave, quickly, and head towards the Boulevard Beaumarchais. She was scared stiff, that was obvious. Has Delarge frightened her? He would definitely not want to go complaining to Delmas, there's much more to incriminate him than there is me. Or he's played some trick, he's made up some story which puts me in the shit.

What's happened to my newfound feeling of peace?

When I pass a news kiosk I ask for a copy of *Artefact* but they have run out of this month's issue. I take three daily papers, two from yesterday and a Sunday paper. A little insert on the front page sends me to the third page. The pages slip from my fingers.

Murder of great art lover.

My head is spinning, I have to put the paper down on the pavement to turn the pages.

A feeling of nausea has swept over me.

The famous art dealer Edgar Delarge, a well-known figure in the contemporary art world, was found strangled to death on Saturday night in his gallery on the Rue Barbette in the fourth Arrondissement. His attacker had cut off Delarge's right hand, which was found several feet from his body by the police. Investigators have not been able to identify any thefts amongst the few valuable pieces he keeps exhibited in his gallery. Two pieces had, however, been damaged: a painting by Linnel – a close friend of the dealer – had been burned, and a Kandinsky had been defaced. When his death was announced and, following a brief enquiry, a journalist from the review Artefact, *came forward to the police to . . .*

Passers-by are turning to look at me, finding it funny seeing someone on the ground trying to pin down the pages of his paper in the wind.

. . . provide information in connection with the murder. The investigators quickly found a link with a case opened by Superintendent Delmas from the crime prevention unit . . .

I wipe my forehead with my sleeve. My eyes skip through the lines and jump from one word to the next without taking in the meaning.

A young man was clearly singled out as the perpetrator of the murder. A former technician at the Coste Gallery, he . . .

I'm hot.

. . . took revenge for the assault in which he lost his own hand by mutilating the man he held responsible for his amputation.

The sentences are merging together, the words are empty. I have to latch onto the end of one line to go on to the right one, the one below.

The young journalist was working on an incriminating article, to be published in May, which would reveal fraud carried out by the dealer. "I just wanted information on the 'Alfonso affair', and I knew he wanted revenge on Delarge,

but I would never have dreamed that he would go that far,"
she told police during questioning. The young man had car-
ried out his own investigation so that he himself could find a
culprit. With help from the journalist, with whom he had
offered to form a "united front" against Edgar Delarge, he
had successfully traced the beginnings of a set-up that dates
back more than twenty-five years and in which the dealer was
already implicated. In 1964, during an exhibition . . .

It's all there. I've forced myself to go right to the
end. My whole story is laid bare here, in four big columns. She didn't forget to tell them anything. The
only bit that's missing is the end. Or the very beginning. The three artists with their plot to eliminate
Bettrancourt. The only element she didn't have.

Edgar Delarge will be buried on Tuesday at the cemetery in
Ville-d'Avray . . .

There are beads of ice-cold sweat down my spine.

According to Superintendent Delmas, the suspect will be
arrested imminently . . .

I mustn't stay here, virtually lying on the ground, with
my nose in the air. On the Boulevard Beaumarchais.

They're looking for a one-armed man.

Who has killed.

Who has cut off someone's hand. It's impossible for
it not to be me. It can only be me. Maybe I did finish
him off, after all, back there on the end of his leash.
And I so wanted to have a second hand. I must have cut
it off, and then, forgotten . . . Béatrice saw him set off,
this madman hungry for revenge, heading towards the
man who had handicapped him in the first place. And
before that, at the private view, everyone saw that same
amputee furiously attacking the same man. And he
must have left tracks, there, at the gallery. Given that
he was there that night. His guilt is even more obvious
than Delarge's death.

And he will be arrested imminently.

It's time to get back on my feet, to walk, to go down to the end of the street and to leave. Not towards the Gare de Lyon, not towards the Rue de Turenne or the maze of streets in the Marais. Nowhere. Arrested imminently. I'm going to escape from the prying eyes of all these people in the street, I'm going to hide my arm, my amputee's arm, the amputee who only understands the law of retaliation, an eye for an eye, a hand for a hand. The papers are saying I have stepped over the boundary ... I thought I had stopped myself on the very brink, right at the edge of the free territories. Briançon was right all along, with his images and metaphors.

Don't leave Paris.

My parents would have preferred hearing I had lost a hand than committed a murder. It would have been so easy to tell them I was one hand short, compared to this unacceptable truth. The police in Biarritz must have been to see them already. They are my only ties in the world, my only possible shelter. "*Someone we can contact,*" the doctor kept saying in hospital. "*No one? Really?*"

How did I manage to live like a foreigner, with my two half-lives, the daytime one and the night-time one? Even Paris feels like the threat of exile to me.

Place Saint-Paul, a Métro station, two possible directions, towards Pont de Neuilly, why not, or Château de Vincennes, why not. A newspaper kiosk stuffed full of papers, a phone booth, people out for a Sunday stroll, a police car speeding towards Bastille.

I won't last long.

I go into the booth, thinking the glass box might cut me off from the comings and goings for a moment. I don't have a diary, just a little square piece of paper

161

with the bare essentials of my few contacts, folded into the sleeve for my travel pass. I have to talk to someone, to plead my innocence. I have to succeed in convincing one person, just one, and I can think of only one.

He likes me. I've never understood why. He's already taken me in once.

"Doctor Briançon? It's Antoine. Antoine Andrieux, I have to see you, I have to talk to you . . ."

"No . . . it's impossible . . ."

"Have you read the papers?"

"When the police searched your apartment they found some notes I left for you. They've asked me about you, my opinion as a therapist, the psychological repercussions of your accident."

"And what did you tell them?"

"What I've always thought. The thing I've always warned you against, your repressed violence, your abdication . . . And all that that can entail in terms of behavioural problems. Why didn't you listen to me?"

"But . . ."

"Go to them, Antoine. It's the best thing to do."

"I didn't kill anyone."

"Listen, they told me to let them know if you contacted me. I'm not going to ask where you are at the moment, I won't tell them you've called, but if you come here I won't have a minute's hesitation. It's the best thing I could do for you. So, go of your own free will. It's important."

His voice has the steady, level-headed ring of someone talking to a psychopath. A precise, rather learned turn of phrase which is enough to turn you into one, if you're not one already. I mustn't let myself fall into that trap. I must stay focused on that last image, the marker pen falling to the ground, the cynical way I left

162

and my satisfied smile, having shamed such a master-piece. That is what happened. I waited a long time before hanging up.

"You know, Doctor . . . I was right to turn down your sessions. When you've slipped right to the bottom of the slope, when you've gone from being a master to being a slave, the only way to get out of the desert is with the long, slow, fiddly trials of everyday life. I've never felt so left-handed as I do today."

I came out of the booth with the square of paper crushed inside my hand.

There are people waiting for me at the buffet restaurant at the Gare de Lyon. I can picture them. Béatrice, sitting down, frightened to death, a couple of men, not far off, sitting outside a café, pretending to look at the departures board, and Delmas, not far away either, hiding in the customs office, and still more, at each exit . . .

Finding another booth, near the Sully bridge, I tried again, and I can't forgive myself for thinking of Véro . . . It only lasted a few seconds, just long enough to hear her stammer in surprise and fear (another one): "you're . . . you're . . ." She couldn't find the word, and I didn't have time to help her, she hung up. And I started to think what she must be thinking, imagining all the hypotheses available to her, principally: I'm a murderer, I've always wanted that painting from the depot, Nico would never have given it to me, I killed Nico. Why not?

Ile Saint-Louis.

Open skies.

I need to find somewhere I can wall myself up alive. Before someone else does it. I think back over the last few years, of all the people I've spoken to. Recently there have been Liliane, Jacques and Coste. Those three must already be telling the sorry tale of the secretive, bloodthirsty picture-hanger they came into contact with every day without suspecting a thing. "We never knew what he did after six o'clock."

What was it that made him catapult out of the gallery after six o'clock as if he were being released from a dungeon?

Well, I know.

*

It took me an hour on foot to get to the Place des Ternes. On the way, I went along the banks of the Seine as much as I could and tried to walk like an innocent man. And I panicked myself. All the way to the Alma Bridge I honestly thought that a man on the run had well-honed techniques, and I was just a novice who could only look at his own feet and who paled at every last siren in the area.

Even so . . . Somewhere in the depths of my conscience weighed down by all the evils of this world, a little blast of hope came and saved me from going under.

I have them. Three or four of them, no more, but that's incalculable. I was their junior, their heir, their child prodigy. They believed in me. They couldn't give a damn about what I did before six o'clock so long as I was there, doing my conjuring tricks with the red and the whites.

They saw me grow up, a shy boy who listened attentively to advice from old men. They all got together to work through the range of shots, depending on their specialities. Angelo told me everything there was to know about striking the ball to get it to do two things at once, until you sent the thing mad. René, with his expertise of the "screw shot", taught me how to get the ball to come back as if, in full flow, it suddenly changed its mind and came back to its exact point of departure. Benoît, who was nicknamed the "Marquise of Angles", told me all the secrets of three-cushion shots. And old Basile showed me everything you shouldn't do, making the balls leapfrog each other, the multiple collisions, the dead ball shots, all the things that won't do you any good but will please the crowd.

Everything that has now been crushed to death under a hundredweight of scrap iron.

They're all that's left to me now. If they shut the door of the academy on me, then the door to prison will be opened wide. And I wouldn't hold it against them, I stole away like a thief and I'm coming back as an assassin. It's asking a lot.

While waiting for the official closing time at eleven o'clock I have forbidden myself any cafés. The Parc Monceau struck me as the only suitable place in the area. I would have liked to lie down on a bench but I forced myself to behave as well as possible, to stroll along in perfect anonymity, just someone getting some fresh air as he eats his sandwich, attentively reading his Sunday paper and trying to work out what sort of shit had managed to shoulder a crime onto him. I didn't prevaricate for very long on that last point. A name came to me very quickly.

In the distance I saw a man in a blue uniform asking people to leave the park. I didn't wait for him to come over before getting up off my bench without making a fuss. From five o'clock till eleven o'clock I walked and walked, all round the Champs-Élysées and the Place de l'Etoile. I can hardly stay awake. René must be picking up his keys now. He has put the balls away in the counter and is calling out to everyone to let them know it's closing time. Angelo is wondering whether his wife has waited up for him in front of the TV, Benoît is suggesting one last swift one to anyone who is interested. Downstairs the green sign is still lit up. My heart starts pounding, perhaps because I've just slipped, perhaps because of them upstairs not expecting me. I've been going round in circles, obeying all the green lights and making detours to use all the pedestrian crossings. Before starting up the stairs I take a deep breath. I've never climbed them so slowly. Three teenagers are coming down, still pumped up and surprised to find that it's already dark. Standing on the threshold of the double doors I press my forehead up to the window to see whether they have already started switching off the lights, or whether there are still one or two die-hards who really don't want to go home.

The pink lamp over table 2 is still on. Angelo is looking out of the window with a beer in his hand. René is putting the covers over the tables. Benoît is playing alone, putting on a bit of performance but no one is watching him showing off. There's that clammy Sunday evening atmosphere. I almost want to leave so as not to disturb their peace. Their slow contentment. Maybe they've already forgotten me. If I didn't feel as if a wanted poster was dogging my every move, I'd be far from Paris by now. Sometimes it's very difficult accepting the decisions we make on principle.

René has noticed a figure the other side of the door. "Closed!" he shouts. I go in. They all look up at me. With my sleeve behind my back, I stop by the first table.

I wait.

Angelo chuckles.

René is trying to find something to say.

"Well, what sort of time do you call this to show up . . .?"

Benoît comes over to me, and Angelo sniggers:

"Hey . . . it's you, pretty boy! You bitch! And what about your poor old friends, here all on their own, beezee worrying . . .?"

He's just the same, with his Italian face and his exaggerated accent. Some things never change on this lowly earth. And there's Benoît, standing right in front of me, pinching my shoulder to check I'm not a fake.

"Is it you, Antoine?"

"Well . . . yeah."

"Well, if it *is* you, then you're a bloody jerk."

Has he read the papers? No, I'd be surprised if he had, he finds it hard enough reading the sports pages.

"Yes, a jerk . . . Are you ashamed of us? Have you gone off to play at Clichy? And what about Langloff? He must have rung ten times!"

The trio slowly gathered round me. If they had wanted to smash my face in, they would have made just the same manoeuvre. I didn't know what to say to them, there wasn't a single word that could explain any of it. I just pulled up my sleeve to reveal my stump. I knew that that would do as an explanation.

"Look quickly because I'm going to put it away."

René, trying to sound sure of himself, was still looking for something to say.

"That's no excuse."

They didn't dare kiss me. We'd never done that. One by one, they held me to them. Like an idiot, I told them I was going to cry, and they laughed at me.

What could I tell them? I admitted to my work at the gallery, and they had trouble understanding even that.

I felt as if I was speaking another language. The only contact René had had with painting was to tape the lid off a chocolate box to a wall because it had a picture of a clown on it. Benoît asked me whether "contemporary" meant "modern". As for Angelo, he just made a point of reminding us that the *Mona Lisa* belonged to Italy and not the Louvre. How could I explain to them that people could kill each other for three red squares on a black background, or three upside-down bowls on three tins of peaches? As I got further into my story and gauged the depth of their scepticism I realized how I should describe it to them: the hand. That was the only thing they had seen. The hand. I had lost it, I wouldn't ever be able to play again, and I wanted to find the man who had done that to me. Simple. End of story, all the rest was just talk, it all boiled down to money like everything else.

When they looked through the article about me in the paper, they got the basics: I was seriously in the shit. Against all expectations, they immediately believed my version of the facts in relation to the other hand, Delarge's hand.

"The guy who did this . . . He wanted people to think it was you, definitely!" said Benoît.

"And it's a bloody good idea!" added René.

"Eeeeven if I was a poleeeceman, I would never guess."

"And where are you going to live now?"

I was eternally grateful to René for asking that.

"I don't know. I've been looking all day. I need to find somewhere for four or five days. I know who did this."

"And what will you do to him if you collar him?"

"I don't know yet."

"Mother of God! No messin' about! If someone do zis to me, I make him eat his hand in ossobuco!"

168

Good idea, Angelo. I'll bear that in mind . . .

René points his finger at me and speaks firmly and definitively: "You're going to stop fucking about, you can stay here, full stop. I'll open up the storeroom for you, and you can sleep on the table covers, you'll manage. During opening hours I'll lock you in, there aren't many nosey people here but there could always be some shit-stirrer. In the evenings I'll close a bit earlier and you can come and get some fresh air on the balcony with us.'

This back room is my haven of peace, a palace of a dungeon, the Hilton of hideouts. It might even delay that imminence. René, keeper of the golden keys, the one who's really taking the risk of harbouring a criminal, doesn't seem to be weighing up the risks. Far be it from me to awaken his suspicions. This is more than a godsend he's offering me, it's my last chance. I wouldn't have lasted two nights outside. I'm not made for this sort of thing, I'm not designed to be a slalom champion and I've never had a knack for running between the raindrops in a storm. That takes some dexterity, and I'm just not dextral any more, I'm fresh out of right hands.

They eventually left in the middle of the night. I didn't miss the fact that René discreetly left one box of balls open, right where I couldn't miss them. He didn't switch the lights off or put the cover on table 2. I don't know what they're hoping for. I really don't. They know as well as I do that there's not a chance.

In the still of the night the room takes on all the majesty of the very first time I saw it. Without the dance of the players and the waltz of the balls, the tables look like empty beds, almost inviting. My footsteps make the wooden floorboards creak. I sit at the counter and sip a beer. Not thinking of anything. Loitering. Slightly unwillingly, I take three balls and throw them onto table 2. I rediscover the delicious sound as they smack against each other. With my hand I roll one of them towards the far cushion and watch it come back, then I do it again, and then again, to pass the time, the time I need to remember. I carried on like that a good while, waiting for the pain.

Which never came, never hacked into my heart.

That must be good news.

I'm almost cured of billiards.

The night was too short, the day too long and the sandwich René gave me even more asphyxiating than the little storeroom. Stuck between my mattress of covers, a forest of chipped cues and a crate of dead light bulbs, I waited for the hubbub of games to die down. The slightest movement created a storm of dust, and I held my nose closed to stop myself sneezing. The papers didn't say anything more, apart from some vague details about the Objectivists' abortive history. I wondered where on earth they could have got my picture from. I worried about that, actually. At about ten o'clock in the evening Angelo came in, wearing a smile like a trapper come to set me free from my snare. When I stepped from that washed-out darkness into the blue darkness outside, I rushed over to the balcony as if I had been holding my breath. I don't know whether it was the confinement, the four floors up, the impression of hunger, the fresh air or the simple fact that Benoît had laid the balls out on table 2, but I suddenly felt dizzy. The balls are waiting for me, the players are watching me, my refusal and their disappointment will undermine the atmosphere.

"I'm not going to play, guys. Don't start," I say between two lungfuls of air.

René comes over to me.

"Never say never . . . I'm sure with time . . . Right, okay, it's not easy to lose your leading hand, but with a good prosthetic you could manage a thing or two."

I see . . . the future champion is dead but the friend is still there. After all, people come to the academy to enjoy themselves and not necessarily to reach the eternal heights of the most perfect game in the world. It's a commendable intention . . . but I still had to bite my lip to stop myself swearing at him.

"That's exactly what I'm afraid of, just doing a thing or two. At the moment I'm fine, I've almost lost the urge to play, but if you keep insisting you'll end up really hurting me."

Benoît has started playing, and Angelo has stopped looking at me.

"Do you want a bite to eat?" René asks.

"No, I wouldn't mind a beer."

"I know why he rifioose to play, old Antonio. It's because he hasn't kept his hand in."

Complete silence. I must have heard wrong. Benoît almost missed his shot.

"You shouldn't say things like that when I'm just about to play, idiot!"

"But it's true, no? Antonio has been dealt a bad hand."

What do I do? Do I laugh or smash his face in? A smile sketches its way onto Benoît's lips.

"Got to hand it to him, he used to play masterfully."

René has gone back to playing, with the others.

"He always knew how to keep the game in hand."

171

I don't understand what's going on any more. They don't usually elaborate on things like this, but . . .

"It would only have been a couple of years before he got his hands on the Championship."

Benoît, very straight-faced, adds to this: "Yup, he'd have seen the competition off hand over fist."

"Nothing underhand about his style, wouldn't you say?"

I listen to them in stunned, defenceless silence. Are they my friends or are they not my friends? They're not leaving me a split second to counterattack.

"He was pretty heavy-handed back there with that art dealer."

"Well, yes . . . and the police nearly got him with the long arm of the law."

The laughter starts bubbling up from every direction, and I just stand there like a prick.

"He wants to lay his hands on the culprit all by himself."

Angelo is trying his best to hold back his laughter. Not for long, just long enough to add: "But, for the billiards, he needs to turn his hand in!"

"Hey . . . did you rehearse this before getting here, or what?" I ask in amazement.

"We just wanted you to try your hand at a thing or two . . ."

"Bunch of arseholes."

"But if you like, we won't force your hand, you know!"

Benoît is holding his sides, the other two are bent double, shaking in spasms.

"And the culprit, he want the hand to hand combat . . ."

I look down at the floor, piqued. And, in spite of myself, I can't help letting out a little snort.

"Do you want me to start handing out punches?" I ask.

"No! Hand on heart!"

That's the final blow. Benoît collapses onto a seat with his arms crossed over his stomach. René is convulsing, no longer able to contain himself. Angelo wipes a tear from the corner of his eye.

Almost giddy with laughing, he comes over to me.

"You don't hate us, do you? We're bastards, no?"

"I've known worse." I said.

The room gradually falls silent again. I go back out onto the balcony with my stomach muscles burning. Nervous laughter, granted, but it's taken the heat out of the situation. I would like Briançon to have seen me a couple of minutes ago. I've accepted the concept that I won't play any more and I can laugh at myself, but not bitterly or cynically. Soon I'll find out whether there is a future for me somewhere. Just one last thing to do, then the police can do whatever they want with me. I'll leave my friends by tomorrow evening. I have no intention of abusing their hospitality. In my little hole today I reconfigured my moral right to revenge, and this time – with the murder I've just inherited – I mustn't stop at anything. No need to have any scruples. When I saw Delarge, on the ground, spewing out his every last hate, I backtracked. I pitied him, not myself. My supplies of rage had gradually run dry. But I'm sure I can come up with one last little spurt. It's like adrenaline – we don't know it's happening, but we still secrete the stuff.

*

René came and released me at the same time as the previous day. The three accomplices know I'm leaving and they're not so full of jokes now.

"You've got stuff to sort out, we know that. Try to come back, one evening, when you're not scared. If we have to start reading crap papers to get news of you . . ."

Who knows when I might be back . . .? I won't come back as an outlaw, it's too uncomfortable, too dusty. I will have thrown off the trappings of a criminal that suit me even less than my own garb as a tramp. I'll come back relaxed, showered, shaved, at peace with myself.

I've asked René to ring the man who isn't expecting me this evening. The man who works at night, to change the colour of his colours. I absolutely knew he would answer the phone, I had a feeling of certainty the minute I came out of my little hideout to go and breathe the night air.

"I'm so sorry, I must have the wrong number," René said.

"Hope your balls roll well!" Benoît called, not really sure why he said it.

I left without saying goodbye, and Angelo followed me onto the stairs. I already told him yesterday he couldn't come with me.

"*Non fare lo stupido*, get into the car, dickhead . . ."

I put my bag on the rear seat and sat next to Angelo. The angel. To avoid the Place de L'Etoile he went along the Rue de Tilsitt – a precaution that amazed me.

"So, when is the final for the Championship actually?"

"Last week. *Bella partita*, the guy from Marseille, he won the title. Langloff he come fourth."

A good position, for a brave last stand.

"What about you, Angelo, didn't you ever sign up for it?"

"I'm not French, for a start. And I would be out in the first round. I don't play billiards for the *competizione*."

"Well, why do you play then?"

"Oh well . . . I . . . *Perche* the baize is green and the balls are red and white. It's the colours of my flag! *Ammazza!*"

We sat in silence for the whole rest of the journey. On the edge of the Parc Montsouris, not far from the Rue Nelson, he stopped the engine and I put my bag on my lap.

"What can I do now?"

"Nothing. You can't help me any more."

"Can I wait downstairs?"

"Don't be stupid. You don't know what I'm going to do yet."

"Are you sure that he is alone?"

"Absolutely sure."

"And do you have to take that bag?"

Actually, no, he's right. There's really only one thing in it that matters to me. I rummage through the old clothes and the papers to get it out. I do it in front of him, ostentatiously, so that he stops wanting to help me. When I have it in my hand, Angelo shudders.

"What are you going to do with that thing? Stop pissing about, Antonio. You're not going to use that fucking thing."

Worried then, Angelo. Just what I wanted.

"I'm getting you out of here, come on, forget about it . . . I have family, in Italia, they will find you a place

175

for a few months, and then we will see, you could leave . . . I don't know . . . put that thing down . . ."

"Do you still want to come with me?"

He doesn't hesitate: "If you've gone mad, I prefer no."

With great difficulty I manage to stuff the thing into my inside pocket. It won't stay there long. I bought it after my convalescence.

"Are you going home now, Angelo?"

"No I'm going back *alla'accademia*. When I play, it calms me down and I don't think about anything else."

And he set off, just like that, without another word. I went up the Rue Nelson, which is no more than a cul-de-sac lined with smart three-storey houses with gardens and rose hedges. At number 44, almost at the end of the street, the general appearance is somewhat different. The garden is abandoned with a shrub covered in dried-out flowers and an abandoned hose-pipe by the rusted gate. There are no lights on in the upper floors but on the ground floor, which is slightly downhill from me, I can make out a glow far away, at the back of the house. The gate is waist high – with two hands I could have climbed over it easily, without making a sound and without getting caught on the spikes. Like a petty thief coming to nick apples. I'm left-handed now but I don't have the background for it.

It didn't creak too much but I left a strip of my jacket on it. There's a little gravel path down the right side of the house, leading to another garden at the back, even more ramshackle than the first. Couch grass and wild ivy have grown up all round a huge bay window with sliding doors that takes up one whole wall on the ground floor. I stood in the corner of the

176

building a long time before making up my mind to look in.

Then I saw, at last.

There are two powerful spotlights converging on a wall. Their unbearably white light illuminates a stagnating mess. A trench carving its way through dozens of tins of paint piled up any old how, most of them closed but all of them dripping with crusty dried paint in a mishmash of colours. Empty, upturned paint pots, piles of lids stuck together for untold ages, crushed tubes, a myriad little glasses full of the same greenish soup, with forgotten paintbrushes in them or left on the floor. A copper basin with more paintbrushes, next to a whole load more glasses and splash marks, I keep seeing more of them, thrown here and there around the room. Jungles of newspapers have invaded every last corner of the room, a carpet of papers splattered with paint and torn by heavy footsteps. Floorboards covered in a jumble of paintings, not one of them identifiable. A huge canvas fitted between the floor and the beams on the ceiling exactly matches the dimensions of the wall. You'd swear it was a fresco. Part of it is already no longer white, on the left hand side I recognize the brushstrokes I saw at the Pompidou Centre.

Crouching in front of it, frozen like an animal about to pounce, I spot him at last. Him. Linnel. Ready for work. He almost had to move for me to recognize a human body in amongst that brightly coloured cataclysm. He too is daubed right up to the neck, with his T-shirt and jeans oozing green and black. I get it, he's trying to lose himself against the rest. Chameleon tactics. He thought I would miss him, camouflaged, motionless, lost in the luxuriance of his own work. He stays there crouching, totally alone, a thousand miles from my prying eyes, perfectly taut and mesmerized by the blank space.

All of a sudden he lies down full length in the morass of newspapers, knocking over a glass of water without even noticing. Then he gets up, in one bound, and dips his brush in a pot drooling with yellow. The brush drips over to a little shelf and dives into a thick layer of white. Linnel stands facing the canvas, arm outstretched.

At that precise moment his hand started to fly.

I saw it twirling through space, darting here and there like a wasp, making scattered dabs of light appear. I saw it flitting in every direction, far from the rest of his body, creating its own anarchic and obvious geometry. I saw it skim airily over a forgotten area, then change its mind, abruptly, and come back to pick up more colour. More feverish than ever, it flew off again in a series of jerking movements, dispensing black arcs in every direction, most of them broken in exactly the same place, going back over some of them to make them smoother or more curved.

Linnel came back to his senses, his eyes scanned the entire room to unearth another, thicker brush. Same mixture, same speed, more gobs on the floor. Back on the canvas, his hand flattened up against it to trace a long strip of colour until the brush ran out of paint. Now streaming with yellow, it started lurching furiously along the same line, skidding off track in places and recovering along the horizon it had just created.

I sat down in the cold grass. I rested my head against the metal upright of the window frame without taking my eyes off that hand which fell back down exhausted for a few seconds, hanging limply by his side with the paintbrush.

Linnel dropped it where it fell, then overturned the pot of white paint, which was almost empty. He took a screwdriver and kneeled down next to another, a big new one. Having ripped off the lid, he mixed the paint with a stick and dunked a wide brush in so that it was gorged with white. Now using both hands, he swept over the entire canvas with an almost transparent veil. I witnessed the metamorphosis as a live show. All of the work so far started a process of rebirth beneath the veil. The dabs that were still wet seemed to blossom, the arcs joined together of their own accord, the trajectory of the dark line stood out against the unicity of the background, and the zigzags, along the edge, all shifted in the same direction, as if to escape the frame.

Linnel lies down on his front, stammering out an absurd gasp. I rest my forehead against the windowpane. I've never seen anything so moving in my life.

But I'll get over it.

I slid one of the French doors open but it took a ridiculously long time for the noise to rouse him. Still, he did deign to look up. He looked me up and down with his empty eyes. I thought I should make the most of his prostrate position to pin him to the ground, but I realized that he had no desire to stand up.

"Already?" he asks, barely even surprised.

He sort of sits up, on one elbow.

"I'm feeling a bit groggy. Would you mind letting me pull myself together for a minute?" he says.

I smiled, remembering that the first time we met he was nothing like so polite.

"If you'd come fifteen minutes earlier you would have disturbed me. You've come to make a fuss, haven't you? To fuck everything up . . ."

179

"The only way to fuck this place up would be to tidy up the shit on the floor a bit."

"What shit?"

I forgot that he was mad. But this time there was no alcohol involved, or irony. We're alone together, without an audience. This evening he isn't the star turn, there are no fans or journalists or buyers. Just me.

"Let's get this straight between us without any dramas. I can't stand dramas," I say.

"The drama's up there on the wall," he says, pointing to the canvas. "The only drama worth anything. I've had my quota for the evening. What do you want? What do you really want?"

First of all I'd like him to stop posturing, wipe off that air of detachment, that relaxed expression. And I know how to go about it: I just have to answer the question, really answer it. Without lying. With one simple gesture. I took out the thing Angelo was so afraid of. Once I had it properly in my grasp, I aimed at a wooden shelf halfway between Linnel and myself. I kneeled down too. And with one sharp blow, I buried the cleaver into it.

He stared at it stupidly, as if trying to see himself reflected in the blade. Very gently, on his backside, he gradually backed away from the cleaver. I took the handle again to ease it out.

"Don't move. Or this horrible thing could land anywhere, wherever luck would have it, and it's not your hand you're in danger of losing."

"You didn't go all the way with Delarge, so . . . why now?"

"I calmed down, it wasn't worth it any more. And, anyway, there wouldn't have been any point in taking Delarge's hand, all it ever does is shake hands with critics and sign checks. In other words, nothing. He was

180

among the nine tenths of humanity who never wonder about the extraordinary tool they have at the end of each arm. Yours has just given me the most beautiful demonstration in the world. A painter at work."

"Did you see?"

"I loved it. You have that gift, the magic key, the one that opens all the doors. The one I've no longer got. God, it would be lovely for my poor left hand to hold your right one. While with the other one – the one that's still inept – you call for an ambulance."

He's got it. He didn't need me to repeat it.

"I could make a call right now . . . To Delmas . . . I could still admit the truth to him . . ."

"And then what? You'd go to prison? And you'd carry on painting. No way. I'd rather you told me how you did it, to Delarge, because I haven't yet chopped off a single hand in my life, I need advice."

He pushes aside two or three glasses so that he can lie down more comfortably. I realize I'm going to have a lot of trouble putting the fear of God into him.

"It's easy, you know . . . I'd been looking for a way to get rid of him and his blackmail for twenty years. That evening he gave me a cry for help, you'd just left. When I saw him sobbing on the floor, slumped there in his own gallery, I realized I'd finally been given an opportunity I couldn't miss. All I had to do was cut his hand off and everyone would obviously think it was you. You're the prick who'd just finished defacing a Kandinsky. You've no idea what you did there. What an irresponsible arsehole . . . you can't do that to the memory of a man who thought painting was everything."

He pauses for a moment.

"And anyway, you've got a bloody cheek, you could have burned the Braque instead of my painting!"

"What blackmail are you talking about?"

"Oh that, I imagine he didn't give you much on that . . . After Bettrancourt died he made it very clear: I would work for him, for life. I was offered a fortune a thousand times by some of the biggest galleries in France."

"What about your two accomplices?"

"Etienne reacted the best way possible, he flew off as fast as he could to the Babylon of the art world that New York had turned into. Contemporary art had switched continents. But I had no intention of leaving Paris. I wanted to paint here at home, in spite of everything, and Delarge gave me the opportunity. Claude, on the other hand, he was in the same boat as me. Delarge congratulated himself when he saw him following in his father's footsteps. Sooner or later that would be useful to him too. The proof in the pudding: Claude couldn't turn down the Alfonso con trick. Tough luck on him, he never dreamed that it would come back to haunt him. Twenty-five years later."

He seems satisfied to have said that.

"Of the two of us, you're the one who's lost it, Linnel. Why were you so friendly with me at that private view?"

"When we saw this one-armed man pitching up at the Pompidou Centre we worked it out straightaway. The man who did that to you was a hired . . ."

"A hired hand, go on, say it. There are plenty more like it. I can *hand*le it."

"Let's say he was one of Delarge's henchmen. He told us about his little performance at the Coste Gallery. I wanted to know what sort of person you were, what you had in you. When you punched Edgar's lights out it gave me confidence. I was completely on your side.

And then I waited quietly for you to go and see him, one to one."

I moved closer to his painting, still keeping a reasonable distance from his head. The smell of paint prickled my nose.

"And what about Morand's painting, *Attempt 30*? Was it really all that dangerous?"

"Delarge, Claude and myself all agreed that it had to be withdrawn from circulation as quickly as possible. Do you want to see it again?"

"Hasn't it been destroyed?"

"Edgar wanted to, but I couldn't. You know ... I understood why Etienne painted it. To remember us, mainly, what we were. And as atonement. Look, it's almost at your feet, in a cloth."

It is lying on the floor, wrapped in a white towel. I unroll it with two fingers, not letting go of the cleaver. I recognize it.

"Even at the Beaux-Arts, Etienne was already fascinated by anamorphic work and miniatures. He could spend weeks on end studying Chinese calligraphy. He even had a thesis project on the missing spots in Dutch naïve painting. I've even kept some little masterpieces here, like a reproduction of Leonardo da Vinci's *Last Supper* on a postage stamp. It's a real gem. Once, going back to an ancient Chinese tradition, he proved he could write a whole poem on a grain of rice. He even wanted to make that his speciality – the invisible, hidden details. He loves that old master painting showing a goblet full of wine, with one drop slipping over the edge."

"Don't know it."

"It was a long time, a very long time, before anyone found out that in that droplet – which is no bigger than a pinhead – the painter had done a self-portrait."

"What?"

"That's the absolute truth. One woman just looked at it in more detail that anyone else. Now, if you come in really close to the very tip of the church spire, you'll see . . . But I don't have a magnifying glass, I'm sorry . . ."

"What would I see?"

"The face of our shame. The features of our own remorse."

"A portrait of Bettrancourt?"

"Yes. Incredibly faithful. And that's not all. If you look closely at the colour you can see that it's covering a text. I'm amazed Coste didn't see that."

"A statement?"

"A confession. Detailed, but still a confession. Obviously sooner or later all this would have come out. Beneath the flaking paint you'd have been able to read it like an open book. He'd anticipated everything, right down to using different types of paint. He was an alchemist, our Etienne. A magician. You do understand that it was better not to leave the thing lying around where everyone could . . . could get their hands on it."

I don't pick up on that. He didn't say it on purpose. As for the mystery surrounding the painting and the urgent need to get it away from close scrutiny, I now understand Jean-Yves's intrigued expression just thirty seconds after it was hung.

"Bettrancourt had the idea for the first *Attempt*, didn't he?"

He smiles.

"Julien always used to say: 'there are only three major art forms: painting, sculpture and the crowbar.' He was already telling us about Rothko and Pollock and about Abstract Expressionism while we were still swooning over the delicate mysteries of Monet's

Déjeuner sur l'herbe. He had plenty to say about studious little people like us, you see really . . . the Objectivists was him, and no one else. It didn't take him long to recruit us."

"And Delarge came and fucked things up."

"Oh, that was just the real world which brought us straight back to something more concrete and palpable. Julien saw him coming right away. But it was easy to reel us in, he came and visited our gallery, Etienne's and mine. He did everything he could to get us to drop Julien. And after a while we ended up wondering whether he was right, especially when we saw what he had to offer us. He portrayed Julien as a sort of fascist who would never let us express ourselves. He was the one who suggested the accident to us."

"What you euphemistically call an accident was a murder good and proper. Don't play with words. Afterwards Morand was filled with remorse and Reinhard was terrified."

"The weirdest thing was the effect that death had on our painting, Etienne's and mine. With him it was all black and with me it was everything else."

"The green of hope."

"No, of decomposition."

"In other words, a hand can do any number of different things, paint, tinker with a car, kill a friend . . ."

He dips his finger in a cup and carries on toying with the damp canvas. There are more and more drips on it.

"You know, it's not new. If you look hard enough you can confuse the history of criminality with the history of art. In the beginning people painted the same way they killed – with their bare hands. Crude art you could call it. Instinct before technique. Then the tool intervened, brushes, sticks . . . people realized how incredibly efficient it could be to have something in their hands. Then the materials became more sophisticated and people started painting with knives. Look at the work of Jack the Ripper. Next, with the advent of technology, the gun was invented. Painting with a gun brought something new and terribly dangerous to it all. Hardly surprising the Americans liked it so much. And now, in the age of terrorism, people paint with bombs, in cities, in Métro stations. It's another concept of the profession. Anonymous graffiti going off at the end of the street."

He wipes his fingers and darts a quick look at the cleaver.

"That's why with that thing of yours there, you're a bit . . . a bit stuck in the past. A weekends-only amateur."

I smiled.

"Look, you're . . . you're not going to use it . . ."

I asked myself the same question two seconds ago.

"I don't think you'll use it, because you know what a hand can mean. You had a golden hand too."

"Where did you get that from?"

"It's blindingly obvious, you said so yourself."

No one knows, no one ever knew.

"It's billiards. The gentleman, as you call him, told me how he nearly came to grief when you smacked him across the face with your pole."

"It's called a cue."

"I understood why you were so obsessive then. But you wouldn't do that to me."

With one sharp blow I split open a brand new pot of paint. A thick blue swell spreads over to his knees.

"If I'd become a deaf-mute or even if I'd lost a leg, I would never have tried to get involved in something which had nothing to do with me. It was bad luck for all of us that it was my hand that got it. Put yours on that shelf."

"If you want, then I won't hesitate."

And he proves it. He makes some space around him, brings the palette within his reach and puts his wrist down on it. Quite calm.

"Go on . . ."

Well played.

Let's say it did me good lugging that cleaver along with me. That's all.

Mind you, there is one thing I'd rather not lug around with me any more: a squad of policemen and my "imminent" conviction for murder.

"Take it away, it'll keep you busy where you're going. Call Delmas now. I know it's late but he wants to finish with this as much as I do."

"But who's going to look after Hélène?"

He said it with no edge of spite or calculation. No malice. Yes, he's right, who's going to look after Hélène . . . ?

For the first time this evening I can feel the fear rising in him.

"Delmas will go and ask her questions," he says, "they'll try and explain that the young Alain, the one who comes and comforts her every Friday evening, that he killed her son in a car crash. She won't survive long with that image in her mind. She'll go off and join Julien in the grave within ten minutes."

"It looks like a foregone conclusion," I say. "Then you will have killed her twice, twenty years apart."

I say that on purpose. It's more violent than slicing with the cleaver. Let him suffer a bit now.

"You don't have to spare me, but can't you spare her?"

"What do you mean? I don't really understand."

"I need time. For years now I've been wanting to get her out of that hole. I'm worried something will happen to her. And I know where to set her up, a little place in the sun for her and her museum. No one will know where she is. I just have to persuade her. To achieve that, including the house move, I'll need a week."

"What? Are you crazy or something? I've got a mother too, and she thinks I'm a murderer too."

"Give me time to go and see her. I want her to have a chance to see me. I don't want to run away from something like this. Just a week . . ."

He gets up, changes his T-shirt and rubs his jeans down with a cloth.

"You are joking, aren't you? Did you really think I would let you find yourself a hideaway in the Seychelles? I must be dreaming . . ."

"Who said anything about that? I just want a week to take care of her. I can't leave her behind. One week."

"Not so much as two minutes."

"I thought so. Is it really too much to ask?"

*

I've waited for him to clean himself with white spirit. Still with the cleaver firmly in my hand, I watched for the slightest false move. He didn't say a word.

His mind is whirring like a madman. The madman he is.

"What if we played for it, for this week?"

"What . . .? What do you mean by 'played'?"

"Played billiards."

"You're in no position to take the piss with me."

"I've never been anywhere near a billiards table in my life, I don't know anything about it, not even the rules. My only asset is my hand. You, though, have the knowledge but not the tool. I would say that evens it out well. I'm sure it would be the ugliest game in the world. But why not?"

I've never heard anything so absurd.

Obscene.

And yet I can see how an idea like that managed to germinate in that half-demented mind. He likes playing with fire, he must have sensed that I've got some settling of scores to do with billiards. And on top of that it appeals to the quirky, detached side of him. To his cynicism. He's got nothing to lose. Seen like that, his suggestion seems almost logical. With a madman's logic. And I've always said that fools should be left their share of mystery.

"If we had a quick test of strength, which of us would have a chance?" he asks.

I honestly can't answer.

"You're crazy . . . it would be like me painting with my feet."

"Well, you'd be surprised actually, there are those who have. There are even blind people who paint, I'm not joking."

"Do you think so?"

"I'm sure."

My mind is reeling.

"Just ten points and a straight game. No cushions. It'll be the ugliest game in the world, you're right. But I don't know if it'll sort our problems out."

"Of course it will. You'll see. I bet you my own hand . . ."

*

He drove, without asking me where we were going. When we reached the Rue de l'Etoile I glanced up towards the balcony. I warned them we were coming without giving any explanations. Angelo was looking out for us. He gave me a little wave as I got out of the car. René didn't try to fathom it when I told him I was coming to play. Linnel isn't faltering: he doesn't give a damn about anything so long as he can paint. So long as Hélène can spend her last days in peace, without tarnishing the memory of him, without being confronted with horror a second time. And why have I accepted his duel? He just managed to awaken something in me. That's all. Yes, it will be the ugliest game in the world, a useless player against a damaged one, to each his own handicap. A nasty compromise. A pathetic equity. I like the ugliness of it – my lack of respect for the green baize might prove that it's lost all its appeal for me now, that I can tear it without any scruples. If I no longer have perfection at my fingertips, I might as well shatter the aura surrounding my remaining regrets. So that I can live without any ghosts, once and for all.

And I want to win, that's the worst of it. Apart from that, it's just a bit of a laugh.

"Nice place," he says, walking into the room. "There's a sort of back-street solemnity about it. Good use of space. Pink light on a green background."

René has closed the shutters on all the doors, even the ones on the ground floor. He's not trying to get to the bottom of this. He just wants to see me pick up the wooden cue again, like Benoît and Angelo. The balls have already been set out on table 2, Linnel is given a cue. I choose one from the rack, any of them will do.

"The idea is to strike one of the white balls so that it hits the other two. That's all there is to it."

"Argh . . . games that can be explained in one sentence are always tough. How many years does it take before you score your first point? Without snagging the baize, I mean."

"That depends on the shots, some take ten minutes, others five years. Watch."

I turn towards Angelo.

"Show us the trick with the bottle."

"Wha'? . . . Oh no . . . issa long time since I did it . . ."

"Don't act the prima donna. Show him. Show us."

I know it doesn't take much to persuade him. He loves doing it, especially when he's asked to. Linnel watches him put his bottle of beer down on the baize, right in the middle, and the red ball on the mouth of the bottle. Then he puts one white ball up against the bottle and the other one in a corner of the table. He positions the tip of his cue downwards, perfectly perpendicular to the baize. A moment's concentration and he gives the white ball a brisk smack. A dead ball shot, to be precise. The sidespin on the ball is so powerful that it spins on its own axis and climbs up the bottle in a fraction of a second, dislodges the red, goes back down and rolls over to touch the third ball in the corner.

That Italian's the only person within these walls who can do it.

Linnel, speechless, looks at Angelo as if he were possessed by the devil.

"You're taking the piss . . . There's some trick . . . Have you had physicists here yet? You've got to do that under scientifically controlled conditions."

"Hey, come on! I'm not a laboratory gueeneepeeg!"

"You, the artist, you wanted to play billiards, didn't you? Don't worry, I can't do shots like that any more.

191

We're bound to be equals then. René, teach him how to hold the cue . . ."

While the boss teaches him the basics, I pick up my cue. The problem is keeping the thing in a more or less straight line. I sprinkle a little talc over the inside of my right elbow and clamp the cue in it, not too tightly so that it can slide backwards and forwards. For every shot I have to lie myself down across the table from my hips up. Not a very graceful position, oppressed: the absolute opposite of billiards. The shots are inevitably shorter, I have to strike harder to adjust the aim. I'm squashed down on the baize, all at an angle, but it works. Just enough to actually play. Benoît, who is standing right next to me, looks away. It's not very beautiful, I know . . . Now he sees why I was reluctant to play again.

Linnel saunters back over, holding his cue like a sword.

"Before playing I'd quite like to take some precautions for the next few days," I tell him. "Let's be clear about this, you're going to sign something for me in front of witnesses, and my friends will keep it safe and warm for exactly a week. If I win the match, you give yourself up within quarter of an hour. And you can be sure my mates will help me accompany you, to avoid any dirty tricks. If I lose it, I go to Delmas and keep my mouth shut for a week to give you time to set the old girl up. I don't recommend running late."

"Either way, I won't stay in prison long."

"Really? Everyone who says that seems to pick up an extra five years."

"It's not the same for me. Look at what happened to the Douanier Rousseau. A true naïf. It was in 1900 or 1907, sometime around then, he trusted a crook, which cost him a prison sentence straightaway. He was very proud of his talent and his paintings and very keen to show his paintings to the warders and the prison director. And he was immediately acquitted on the grounds of diminished responsibility."

"No?"

"Yup."

"I wish you the best, then. In terms of diminished responsibility, you've got a chance. First to ten, then, no more. With every point, you get to play again. Don't forget what's at stake. You start."

René comes closer, Angelo stays over by the scoreboard, chalk in hand. Benoît still can't make up his mind whether to watch or not, and slips quietly off to the balcony. Linnel is shaking slightly and admits he feels completely lost.

"Bend your knees a bit, your bodyweight has to be evenly distributed," offers René.

As his opening shot he miscues, the tip skids off the ball and lands against the baize, almost tearing it. Then, bracing my body towards the balls, I do almost the same thing.

"Do you think there's any point going on?" Linnel asks me.

"More than ever."

Quarter of an hour later, no visible improvement. We're still at 0–0. I'm like one of those old men still trying to walk as he did in his prime. Suddenly, having spent a good while thinking, Linnel plays a shot. An easy one, granted, the two balls that need touching are almost stuck to each other. His sets off rather lamely but goes and brushes gently past the other two. A simple point but it has the advantage of being the first. He gives a little cry and misses the next shot, which is even easier. René comes closer still and tries to catch my eye. Far away, in the dark, Benoît turns his head towards us. Angelo writes the number one in Linnel's column. I score another, just after him.

It's 3–6 to me. Linnel is catching up, he is getting more and more confident but I can see what's wrong with his shots. He hits right in the middle of the ball and far too hard.

"You won't do this one by thumping it like that. Just skim the red, and yours will go off all on its own."

Angelo can't stand still and René kneels down so that his head is level with the table. I've never seen them so nervous.

Linnel asks, "Will you go and see Hélène when she's out in the country?"

"Play . . ."

7 to him.

"This time put a bit of left sidespin on the ball, it will come off the cushion and touch the right of the red. Don't worry about anything else."

He respects my instructions to the letter. His ball comes to a halt, kissing the red. He closes his eyes. It's as if I'm playing for the first time myself all over again. The others, who are used to watching matches between real masters, think it's fantastic. This mad game has become an ode to personal bests. The struggling cripple and the non-believer just discovering the faith.

"Come on, get a second point while you're on a roll, it's not a difficult one."

I show him how to go about it. His hand holds so

much promise. Benoît, mesmerized, watches in the distance.

Linnel tries to imitate my position as best he can. He's starting to look like that metal portrait of himself from '62.

He plays the shot.

He shouts for joy.

"Tell me, Linnel. Tell me who that gentleman really is. And whether I'll ever have the good luck to see him again some day."

He's no longer there, off in other spheres.

"No one knows who he really is. Delarge wouldn't have been able to tell you either. He was used as a forger sometimes, but I think he had other ambitions. Then something forced him to disappear into the shadows, anonymity and lies. Everything Edgar was offering him. The only thing I've managed to find out is that he has *Les Demoiselles d'Avignon* tattooed on the top of his left shoulder. Hey, which direction should I be trying to spin this one?"

"Do whatever feels right."

A Picasso reproduction on his shoulder . . .

I don't think he'll get away from Delmas a second time. It won't be an interrogation he'll be subjecting the gentleman to . . . but a valuation.

8 all.

His ball sets off, straight for the target.

We're all there, hypnotized.

I close my eyes the better to hear the collision.

8

For a moment I've stopped listening to the lulling music of the surf.

The sea brought me back to life after a week in jail. Old Hélène is safe now. Linnel was punctual. While I wait till nine o'clock on September 3 for the next stage of the case, I've been granted a few weeks when I can forget it all somewhere between the deep blue of the sea and the azure blue of the sky. But it hasn't taken long for my sun-lounger to get on my nerves. Before the summer season hit I swam a couple of times, completely alone. Preoccupied . . . but still serene. Or almost. I very soon felt slightly anxious at the prospect of so many long slow days to come. But that's also what I like about Biarritz.

I'm in the bedroom at the top. The veranda has undergone a subtle transformation over the weeks. It's become a sort of no man's land that even my father doesn't dare cross.

"Are you coming and having this cup of tea or not . . .?"

"Coming!" I say with no intention of actually doing so.

I've spent too much time concentrating on this thing. And just now, after a good hour of prevarication, I can feel something coming. Nothing dramatic, no, just a little door opening, in the right-hand corner of the picture. A few trails of colourwash that suggested some sort of order to me. I mustn't mess it up.

My left hand is applying itself as best it can. It's being very patient too. I can feel it going along with me so wholeheartedly. My partner.

I've got so much time. I so badly want bright, light colours and gentle movements. And perhaps, one day, some skill. Who knows?

"Hey come on, your green period can wait another fifteen minutes. The tea's going cold."

He wants to talk, my old man. He's intrigued by my daubing. He didn't turn a hair when I asked for a corner of the veranda to set up a canvas, then two, then a basin of water and a tarpaulin, and a couple of paintbrushes, then three. He never comes and disturbs me. I like unfinished things, he says. They, my parents, they're just happy to know that I'm still like the person they used to know. But they've kept the newspaper cuttings all the same.

The old man comes over towards me and doesn't even try to sneak a look at the transparent colours splurging from my paintbrush.

Colourwash. Colourwash. Colourwash . . .

He puts the cup down and moves away. Back on his sun-lounger, he asks me: "What are you doing? Are you looking for something? Are you having fun? Is this serious?"

"Yes, I'm having fun. Yes, I'm looking for something. No, this isn't serious. It's not creative, it's not artistic, it's not symbolic, it's not full of meaning, it's not complicated, it's not particularly beautiful or particularly new."

He doesn't seem convinced.

"Yeah . . . but you're still painting."

Yes. Maybe. Well, anyway, one thing's for sure. I'll never show him what I've got before my eyes, now, at this precise moment.

I hear him laughing, close by.

"Dad, in your opinion, what colour would you say doubt was?"

"White."

"And remorse?"

"Yellow."

"And regret?"

"Grey, with a hint of blue."

"And silence?"

"You'll have to work it out for yourself . . ."